The Last Roundup

Other Avalon Books by B. A. Collier

MAVERICK TRAIL
ONE FOOT IN THE STIRRUP
TROUBLE AT CROSSED FORKS
MUSTANGS FOR MONTANA
MONTANA GRAVES
THUNDER OVER THE RANGE

THE
LAST ROUNDUP

———∽⃝⃝——

B. A. Collier

AVALON BOOKS. [c 1988]
THOMAS BOUREGY AND COMPANY, INC.
401 LAFAYETTE STREET
NEW YORK, NEW YORK 10003

Br. Colleg

ω

PRINTED IN THE UNITED STATES OF AMERICA
BY HADDON CRAFTSMEN, SCRANTON, PENNSYLVANIA

The Last Roundup

Chapter One

"**L**ook out, Luke!"

I looked around wildly. I'd been jogging along with my mind sort of drifting, but that yell of Clay's had me wide-awake in a second. The only problem was that I couldn't see what he meant. Liz skittered uneasily as I jerked her around, trying to see where the danger was.

And then we both saw it. There was a steer the size of a small house coming at us, his head down, his eyes wild, foam lathering his flanks. He didn't look like he was much more than ten feet from us, and I figured I'd better start saying my prayers.

It was a good thing that Liz was thinking a little quicker. She jumped to the side just as the crack of a rifle sounded almost in my ear. The steer shuddered like he'd been poleaxed, and his legs sprawled every which way, but he was going so fast that he didn't really fall until he'd

1

gone right through the spot where Liz and I had been standing only seconds before.

Liz stared at the steer for a minute, then snorted and shook her head, convinced that he wasn't dangerous anymore. I shook my head too, but it was more to clear it than anything else.

"What's the matter with you, Luke?" Clay asked, riding up beside me and shoving his rifle back in its scabbard. "You've been acting half asleep all day. You're going to end up dead if you don't wake up."

He sounded mad and I guess he was. That steer wasn't ever going to get to market now, and with prices the way they were, that meant maybe thirty-five dollars out of our pockets. He hadn't hesitated to shoot it, but he also figured it shouldn't have been necessary.

I shrugged helplessly. I didn't know what was wrong. I hadn't been able to keep my mind on anything all day, and it didn't seem to make any difference how hard I concentrated.

"I don't know," I told him. "I guess I'm tired."

That was pretty feeble and we both knew it. We were all tired, but there was no reason for me to be any more tired than anyone else.

Surprisingly enough, Clay nodded. "Yeah, I guess you are," he said. "I've been noticing it since yesterday. You sleeping all right?"

"Fine. Just not long enough."

He peered at me more closely and got a sort of surprised look.

"You want to wipe a little of that dust off your face, Luke?"

"Huh?"

He pulled his neckerchief off and reached for his canteen. "You remember those Weaver kids, Luke? You know, the ones you visited and left Liz's foal with before we left on the drive?"

"Yeah, what about them?" I said crossly as he started scrubbing at my cheek with the dampened cloth.

"You remember how you told me the youngest one was sick?"

"Yeah, sure. He had measles."

"Well, just as a guess, I'd say you do too."

"You're kidding!"

"Nope. Under all that dust you've got as nice a set of spots as a person could want. How'd you happen to get this far in life without getting measles before?"

I looked at him suspiciously. "You wouldn't by any chance be thinking this is funny, would you, Clay?"

"Now, Luke...."

"Because if you are, you can just—"

"Take it easy, Luke," he said soothingly. "You're just not feeling too good. Why don't you get back to camp? We've nearly got the herd bedded down, anyway."

I glared at him for a while, but the truth was that I was just too tired to do anything but what he suggested. I was lucky I hadn't been killed, and there wasn't any sense in pushing my luck any further.

I guided Liz away from the herd to where Cookie had the chuck wagon set up.

"You're too early," he snapped. "There won't be anything ready for another fifteen minutes."

"Who cares?" I muttered, sliding out of the saddle.

"Who cares?" he repeated in a shocked voice. "What's the matter with you? You always care about food."

He took a closer look, then backed away hastily. "You've got spots all over your face," he said accusingly. "Is that measles? If it is, you can just stay away from me. I've never had measles and I don't intend to start now. As far as I'm concerned—"

"Cookie, will you shut up?" I groaned. Whether it was just because Clay had told me about the spots, I don't know, but I was feeling worse by the minute. "All I want to do is lie down and go to sleep. Now toss me my bedroll and then leave me alone."

He gave me a nasty look, but he pulled my

bedroll out of the wagon and threw it to me. I staggered off a way to the edge of the campsite, spread it out, and crawled in. It wasn't until then I realized that I'd just left Liz standing there with her bridle and saddle on.

I sat up, wondering if I could possibly get my boots on again, and then saw that Cookie was unsaddling Liz. Maybe he wasn't quite as mean as I'd always figured, I thought, and collapsed back into my bedroll.

I closed my eyes, figuring I'd drop right off, but after fighting to keep awake for most of the day, now I couldn't seem to get to sleep. It didn't matter which way I turned, something ached, or a stone was sticking into me, or something. After what seemed like a couple of years, I just gave up and opened my eyes.

"You awake?"

I turned my head and saw Clay sitting there beside me.

"Yeah," I admitted. "I guess I am."

"We've got a little problem, Luke."

"What's that?" I asked with a lot less interest than one of the owners of an operation should have.

"I've been asking a few questions. As far as I can tell, I'm the only man with this drive who's ever had measles."

I blinked in surprise. "Are you serious? I thought everyone but me got measles."

"So did I," he said glumly. "Well, they probably will now."

I twisted around a little, trying to find a more comfortable way to lie. Then I gave up.

"You want anything?" Clay asked.

"Not unless you've got a new body stashed away somewhere."

"Fresh out," he said regretfully. "Look here, Luke. I figure we've got maybe another day or two before the others start breaking out. It probably took a little while for you to get contagious."

"Probably. That doesn't help a lot, does it?"

"Maybe. Sanford Junction is another day up the trail. That's a pretty fair-sized town."

"What'd you have in mind?"

"Picking up another crew."

"Huh?"

"Look, the price of beef is up. We don't know how long it will stay up, but chances are the later it gets, the lower the price will go. We can't afford to waste time. I think I should leave you fellows to have measles in peace and keep moving. You could catch up later."

"I could, but what about the others? We don't really need two crews."

"We'll send 'em back to the ranch. I was a little worried about leaving that place so shorthanded, anyway."

"All right," I said. "It's okay with me, just as

long as you give me a decent map. I don't want to wander all over the place looking for you."

"Don't worry," he said with a grin. "I'll leave a blaze on every tree."

He went to get his supper and tell the crew what had been decided. Meanwhile, I lay there wondering how our luck had gotten so bad. This was the first year since starting the C Bar L that we had decided to drive our cattle to market ourselves. Other years we'd combined trail herds with two other ranchers in the area, and each spread had sent a couple of hands along with the herd.

This year had been different. For one thing, the early-season prices looked like they'd be the highest ever. For another, Hacker Phillips was sending a lot more cattle than usual. By the time we'd finished picking our herd he still wasn't nearly ready to start driving. We'd all talked it over. Clay and I wanted to start driving and try for the big prices, but the others thought we should wait until Hacker was ready.

Once we'd decided to drive early, we'd also decided that we'd better go ourselves. Only one of our hands had much experience driving a trail herd, and he wasn't all that eager to do it again. He'd been in charge of the ranch before when we were away, so we weren't worried about that, and I suppose the truth of the matter was that we wanted to do something different for a while. That would have been fine, but just before we left, Clay's best girl, Breen Ryan, had finally said yes, which meant that the sooner we got back, the happier Clay would be.

It didn't take a clear head to realize that my case of the measles was going to slow us down quite a bit. Now, if I just hadn't thought it would be a good idea to leave that foal with those kids, none of it would have happened. I shifted around and wondered if I might be able to get to sleep if I tried eating something. I guess I was still thinking about it when I fell asleep.

Chapter Two

It took us close to two days to reach Sanford Junction, and we were pretty uncomfortable by the time we got there. Clay had been a little off on his guess, and Cookie was starting to come out with spots by the next morning. The other cowboys joined us one by one, and if nobody else seemed to feel quite as miserable as I did, they still didn't seem to feel like pushing those cattle the way Clay wanted them to.

I spent a lot of time riding on the wagon with Cookie, since I seemed to end up on the ground pretty often whenever I got on a horse. That was uncomfortable for both of us. Cookie blamed me for his spots and whined about it the whole time, so after a while I'd make another try at staying on a horse. Finally Clay got tired of picking me up and told me if I didn't stay in the wagon, he'd tie me to it.

Still, we finally got to Sanford Junction, and by the time we did, everyone was more than ready to go along with Clay's plan to leave us there until we were better.

We got the herd bedded down, and then Clay came over to where I was propped against a tree directing the operation.

"You want to wake up a minute, Luke?" he said, poking me in the shoulder.

I opened my eyes and glared at him.

"Luke," he said soothingly, "I'm going into town now. As soon as I find three or four men, I'll get right back out here, and then you fellows can go get yourselves someplace to stay."

"Won't they all get measles if you bring 'em out here?" I asked.

"Not a chance. As long as I live, I'm never going to hire another man who hasn't already had measles."

He sounded a little bitter, but I couldn't really blame him. Not only had he been moving the herd practically single-handed for the last day and a half, but he'd been doing all the cooking too. That was probably why we were all half starved, but he'd done his best.

"Fine, Clay," I told him. "I'll keep an eye on things here until you get back."

"Luke?"

"Yeah?"

"Don't you think you could do that better with your eyes open?"

He didn't wait for my answer.

He got back about four hours later with three of the toughest-looking hands I'd ever seen. I'd have been a little doubtful about hiring them myself. They looked like they chewed horseshoe nails for breakfast. On the other hand, I didn't have much doubt that Clay could handle them.

"I really wanted four," Clay told me, "but maybe I can pick up another one farther along."

"Yeah," I said, "and if not, it shouldn't be all that long before I catch up."

"I hope not, but don't do anything stupid, Luke. Wait till you're really okay. I haven't much liked the way you've been looking the past two days."

"It can't have been as bad as I've felt. Don't worry, I'll stay put until I feel better."

"Better yet, stay put until the doctor says it's all right to go."

"Doctor?"

Clay took a deep breath. He'd known right along I was going to give him a hard time about this.

"That's right—doctor. Now, you look here, Luke. Never mind the fact that you sure as blazes look like you need a doctor, it's not the easiest thing in the world to find someplace for five guys with the measles to stay."

Well, he sort of had me there. You couldn't just pile us all into the local hotel.

"Anyway, I found this doctor who has a little infirmary, and he agreed to look after the lot of you and let you stay there until you're feeling better."

"Fine," I said, not really feeling like fighting a losing battle. "Can we afford this?"

"What—the doctor? Sure. He won't cost all that much."

"No, not the doctor," I snapped. My temper was still pretty short. "Look, I imagine these fellas you hired have only one horse apiece, right?"

"Yeah."

"Well, you're going to need the whole remuda, then. Which means that we've got to figure out some way of getting our hands back to the ranch."

"I thought about that," Clay said. "You'll have to buy them horses when they're ready to leave."

I winced. "Isn't that going to be pretty expensive?"

"We can sell the horses again back in Braxton if we want to."

"I know, but will that leave us enough cash for the drive?"

He nodded. "I brought more than I thought we'd need, and we can always sell a couple of head off if we have to. The closer we get to the railhead, the higher price they'll bring."

"Okay. Give me what you think I'll need for the doctor and food and horses and such, and I'll do the best I can."

Clay nodded. "I'll ride into town with you and bring back the horses."

"Don't forget to bring halter ropes," I reminded him. "We'll need to keep our saddles."

"Right. You going to take Liz? Nobody else here can ride her."

I hesitated, then shook my head. "I guess not. She won't like it if I leave her in a corral full of strange horses. I think I'll keep Binny, though. No sense in buying another horse for myself when I'll be rejoining the herd."

Clay agreed with that. He wouldn't have let any of the new hands ride Binny, anyway. Binny needs a real gentle hand, and those three didn't look like they had one among 'em.

"All right," he said. "Let's get the others and ride."

He herded us all into town to the infirmary, introduced us to the doctor, and left. The doctor, who was a crusty old-timer named McReady, pointed us all at cots, dumped some nasty-tasting stuff down our throats, and left us to the first good sleep that most of us had had in days.

It had been only about noon when we got

there, but I slept right around the clock and spent most of the next day dozing. When I opened my eyes the morning after that, I felt a whole lot better and hungry enough to eat my saddle. I looked around, but the other cots were empty.

"Finally awake, are you?" McReady asked from the doorway.

I nodded. "I guess so," I said. "Got anything to eat?"

He came over and peered at me closely. "Those spots are almost gone already. German measles."

"Huh?"

"German measles. The spots are redder and it doesn't last as long. Just don't try to do any reading."

"Why not?"

"Because I said not to," he snapped.

"How long before I can get out of this bed?"

"Any time you want to as long as you have the sense to come back to it when you get tired. If you take it easy for three or four days, there's no reason you shouldn't leave then."

"Does that mean I can get dressed and go get some breakfast?"

"I don't see why not. Try the hotel. That's where the rest of your crew is."

Half an hour later I was working my way through a plateful of eggs. It was hard work

and I realized that I wasn't as hungry as I'd
thought. In fact, I was almost ready to call it
quits when the door of the hotel dining room
opened and in walked a big, cheery, good-look-
ing redhead with a smile for the whole world. I
think maybe I hated him on sight. That much
good nature just isn't natural.

He looked around the room, and then he
spoke in a voice that filled the place right up
and drew every eye: "Any of you gentlemen
own that nice-looking Arab cross out there?"

"I do," I said.

He walked over to the table we were sitting
at and held out his hand. "Cort Hanson," he
announced.

I took his hand a little reluctantly. I couldn't
recall ever having disliked anyone more without having a pretty good reason, and it was
making me a little nervous.

"Luke Johnson," I told him. "What can I do
for you?"

"I've got a little proposition for you," he
said. "I like the look of that horse."

"I do myself. But he's not for sale if that's
what you're getting at."

"Not exactly. I'd never try to buy a horse on
the way he looks. When I buy a horse I have to
know he's the best around."

"And how do you do that?" I asked skeptically.

"A little contest."

"You mean a horse race?"

"That's it," he told me with another grin. That man smiled too much. "Only not an ordinary horse race. This is more a winner-take-all horse race."

"All what?"

"All the horses."

"Are you crazy?" I asked him. "You actually get people to take you up on an offer like that?"

"What's the matter? Don't you think your horse could win?"

"How do I know? I've never seen your horse run. Anyway, Binny's a good horse and I like him. I wouldn't want to lose him even if he is slower than your horse. And frankly, if he's slower, I don't see what you'd want with him. Besides," I said as a thought suddenly hit me, "if my horse is faster, you don't get him. So you don't end up with the fastest horse unless you've already got him."

He laughed. "Most people don't catch on all that fast," he admitted. "Actually, so far I have had the fastest horse. Which means I've ended up winning quite a number of other horses, most of them pretty good. I guess yours isn't going to be one of them, though."

"Nope."

"I'd still like to see him run. Say, twenty dollars?"

I started to shake my head, but when Cookie jabbed me in the ribs, I figured it meant that the others were willing to put up part of the stake.

"All right," I said, "but not today."

"No, I hear the lot of you got dropped off here with the measles by your trail boss."

"That's right," I said, not seeing any need to mention that Clay was my partner, not my boss. "How about the day after tomorrow?"

"Suits me. There's a track marked out near the school. How about one o'clock?"

"We'll see you there."

He smiled again and turned away, and I looked at the four faces at the table grinning at me.

"All right," I said. "If the four of you don't come up with half the stake, you're going to be walking back to the C Bar L."

Chapter Three

It's a funny thing about horse races. At least half the people you talk to don't approve of them, but everybody watches them. Things were no different with this horse race. All the men in town were there, but so were all the kids, all the saloon girls, all the old maids, and most likely all the ministers.

I was there too and feeling pretty good for a change. My last spot had disappeared the day before, and Dr. McReady had said I could leave the next day. Meanwhile, the sky was blue, the day was warm, and there was a horse race.

Someone had gone to a lot of trouble to fix things up nice. The track itself was just an oval of dirt, but little red pennants had been stuck up on sticks all the way around the inside edge of the track, and there was a string with more pennants for the finish line.

I rode Binny out onto the track where Cort

Hanson and his horse were already waiting. This was my first chance to size up his horse, and I've got to say that the animal looked good. He was a rangy bay and pretty clearly there was some thoroughbred blood there. Binny was maybe a hand shorter and a lot more compact. Still, if Hanson's horse was as good as he looked, then it ought to be quite a race.

Binny pricked up his ears at all the excitement. He hadn't done much racing, but he liked to show off and he could tell this was a good chance for it.

"Ready to lose your shirt, Johnson?" Hanson asked with his usual big smile.

"I'm ready for just about anything but that," I told him. "Who's going to start this shindig?"

"The sheriff said he'd oblige," Hanson told me. "Here he comes now."

The sheriff was a little round butterball with a cheerful face and surprisingly shrewd eyes. I had a feeling that it might be a mistake to discount him if I'd been planning anything on the wrong side of the law.

"All ready, gentlemen?" he asked. "Those look like two real nice horses you have there. I'm just a little disappointed that none of our homegrown talent has decided to join in, but I suppose this is in the nature of a match race.

Well, take your places, gentlemen, and we'll
get this little race started."

I was surprised to find that Hanson wasn't
from these parts either, but it didn't seem too
important. I eased Binny up next to the bay
and tried to settle him down a little before the
start. He was all set to go, and he didn't much
care where. Not like Liz, I thought with a grin.
She'd been in plenty of races, and she didn't
waste any energy before the start. If it had
been Liz standing there, you'd have thought
she was trying to decide whether to go right to
sleep or have a little snack first.

"On your mark!" the sheriff said, pulling his
gun from his holster.

I took a quick sideways look at Hanson to
see how his horse was settling down. Not a lot
of nerves there, it seemed. Just a little mouth-
ing at the bit.

"Get set!" The gun was raised and pointed to
the sky. "Go!"

There was a crashing boom, and Binny took
off like a scared cat down the track. He wasn't
gun-shy, but he didn't exactly like to have one
going off in his ear, either.

Hanson had gotten off to a fast start too, and
in a second the two of us were running neck
and neck. The race was set for a mile, and I
started wondering what the best way to run it
would be. I hadn't done too much planning be-

forehand since I didn't know anything about the horse we were running against. Hanson had suggested the distance, so I didn't imagine that the horse was a sprinter.

Hanson let his gelding out another notch, and the two of them edged by us. Binny pulled on the reins, not much liking to see the other horse ahead of him, but I held him back. I wanted to see whether Hanson would be content just staying ahead of us or whether he'd try to open up a lead.

He went for the lead. That probably meant he wasn't sure that his horse could handle a burst of speed from us at the end, so I decided to keep Binny about six lengths back until we'd gone three-quarters of the way around. That ought to leave him plenty of time to cover the ground between us and them and then take the lead.

So that's what I did. I don't think Binny was very happy about it, and the people who'd positioned themselves around the track didn't seem to think it made much of a horse race, but I was satisfied with my strategy.

Or at least I was until I got ready to make my move. No sooner did I start to pick up the pace a little than Hanson did the same thing. I had a sudden, uncomfortable feeling that I'd been suckered. Hanson had wanted me to think his horse was a stayer who'd used up all his strength getting out in front at the beginning. I'd been content not to push him for most of the race, thinking I could overtake him later. Now his horse had had a nice easy race and was six lengths ahead with plenty of steam left.

Well, Binny had plenty of steam left too, I thought, and it was just possible that he was fast enough to make up for my bad judgment.

I leaned over and gave him his head. It was what he'd been waiting for. He flattened out and tore down that track, the wind whipping his mane back against my face so that I could barely see.

Hanson had started pushing his horse too, but we were moving up on them steadily and I started thinking that maybe there was enough time left to catch them.

Evidently, Hanson thought so too, because he looked back toward us and this time he wasn't smiling. He brought his hand up and gave his bay a smack. But it didn't really help. That gelding was going as fast as he could.

As if to underline the fact, Binny picked up a notch as if he were just hitting his stride and went sailing past them, just seconds before we reached the finish line.

The crowd seemed to like that pretty well. This was more the sort of race they'd had in mind, and they were all yelling and slapping each other on the back and grinning. I pulled

Binny to a walk and then reined him up. I looked around. Hanson may not have been grinning as broadly as usual, but he didn't really look like a man who'd just lost a horse race, either.

He rode over beside me. "That was some horse race, Johnson," he said. "I don't suppose you'd like a rematch, would you? Not that it'd do me a lot of good from the looks of things. I'd say your horse is just plain faster than mine."

He held out his hand and I shook it.

"I don't suppose that I could interest you in selling that horse, could I? I could sure use an animal like that."

"Afraid not," I told him. "I've got a few uses for him myself."

"I had a feeling you'd feel that way," he said. "Well, if you change your mind, let me know. Meanwhile, I'm buying over at the saloon if anyone's thirsty."

That got a pretty good reaction from the crowd, and everyone drifted in the direction of the saloon. The sheriff stopped only to give me back my twenty dollars plus the twenty dollars I'd won, and then he headed that way too. I don't know whether he thought he needed to keep an eye on the crowd or whether he wanted one of those drinks himself.

"You coming, Luke?" Cookie asked.

"I don't think so," I told him. "I'll cool out Binny a little and then go back to the infirmary. If I'm leaving tomorrow, I want to be rested up."

"All right, see you later."

"Why don't you take your half of this?" I suggested, holding out twenty. "After all, you boys are staying on for another day or so. It won't make too much difference what shape you wake up in tomorrow morning."

"Not to you, maybe," he said a little coldly as he took the money. "Anyway, we'll see you later."

I walked Binny around until he'd cooled out okay, wondering if Hanson had just skipped that with his horse or if he'd given some kid a nickel to do it for him. After that I headed back toward the livery stable and got Binny settled into his stall. He was still looking pretty pleased with himself, so I gave him an extra helping of oats before I headed back to the infirmary to get a little nap.

I'd decided to get an early start in the morning, but it turned out to be even earlier than I'd intended. Maybe it was the nap I'd taken, but I woke up around four and it was pretty clear to me that I wasn't about to get back to sleep. Since I was all packed up and my stomach was telling me that it was way too early for breakfast, I decided that I might as well start right out.

I gathered up my saddlebags and such and crept out as quietly as I could. The others knew I was leaving, and I didn't see any sense in waking them up if I could help it.

The first faint lightening of the sky had started as I stepped out into what little was left of the night. It was cool and quiet, and far off in the distance I could hear the faint crowing of a rooster.

I headed toward the livery stable, walking quietly. This was the time of morning when it's easiest to wake up almost anyone, and people wakened out of a dead sleep are likely to want to know why.

There were two or three horses in the corral at the stable, and a little to my surprise they looked wide-awake. One of them snorted and trotted over to the fence to see if I was planning to give her something to eat. When she saw that I wasn't she looked disgusted and turned away.

The door of the stable was standing ajar, which seemed a little unusual to me, and as I peered through it I saw that I was right. There was someone in there, and he was saddling a horse.

There were just two things wrong with that.

The first was that he was doing it in the dark. The second was that it was *my* horse.

"You want to hold it right there, mister?" I said, pulling my revolver from its holster.

I guess he didn't. He sort of cursed and jumped at the same time, and then a bullet went whistling past my head.

I didn't take much time to consider that. I just slammed the door shut and hit the ground. The fact was that I couldn't see all that much in there and I didn't really want to put a bullet into a horse by accident. On the other hand, the sky was light enough so that the doorway showed up pretty clearly to him and I didn't want to be silhouetted in it.

I didn't know what move that left for me to make. Still, that shot was likely to bring company and it was going to be on my side, so I could afford to wait.

I guess the other guy figured the same thing. Just as the first lamps were being lit in nearby windows, I heard a commotion on the other side of the stable and then the sound of hoofbeats retreating into what was left of the darkness. I ran around the building, hoping to get a clear shot, but there were too many buildings and he already had another one between me and him.

The sheriff came racing up as I went back around to the door.

"What's going on here, Johnson?" he asked breathlessly.

"That's a pretty good question," I admitted. "I came out here to saddle up and get an early start, and there was someone getting my horse ready for me. When I tried to thank him, he took a shot at me, then took off out the back."

"Great!" the sheriff said in disgust. "That's just what we needed around here—a horse thief. Must have been someone who liked the way that race went yesterday."

"Doesn't seem too smart, though," I said. "There can't be more than two or three people in town who wouldn't recognize Binny after that race."

"Well, maybe a lot of thieves aren't that smart," the sheriff pointed out. "Or maybe he wasn't planning to stay around all that long. I guess we'd better go and make sure the horse is okay."

We went into the stable, and Binny was standing there, calm as you please. I walked over and took him by the bridle. He nuzzled my arm just like I'd been the one who'd saddled him up and then taken a shot at something. The starting gun at the race yesterday had made more of an impression on him than this had.

"Well, you're beautiful," I told him, "and you're fast, but you sure ain't very smart."

The sheriff sighed. "I suppose you want to get started?"

"You have some objection to that?" I asked in surprise.

"None at all. Chances are I won't be able to find out who did this since he didn't get the horse. So it won't do any good to keep you here to press charges."

"I wouldn't think so," I agreed. "I didn't get a look at him."

"Then I'll just advise you to keep an eye on your back trail for a while, in case he decides to try again."

"Thanks a lot, sheriff. He'll have a harder job next time."

By then quite a crowd had gathered. I decided to finish saddling Binny while the sheriff got rid of them. Fifteen minutes later I was heading out of town.

Chapter Four

I rode in off the broad sweep of prairie to where the trail herd had set up camp next to the small muddy stream. Looking around the camp, I wondered what in tarnation could have happened. Trail camps aren't always all that neat, but this one looked like a total disaster. The chuck wagon was on its side and everything that had been in it was scattered over half an acre. As for the herd— Well, if there was a cow anywhere within a mile, I couldn't see her.

Trail herds have been known to stampede, of course, and they did it pretty often, as a matter of fact. It was possible that there'd been a stampede here, but somehow I didn't believe it. Things were scattered but they weren't really flattened, and that's how they would have been if eight hundred or so cows had trampled over them. Once I'd decided that, I thought it might be a good idea to figure out what had happened. I gave Binny a little nudge and moved away from the center of the camp in the direction I figured they would have staked out the remuda. Once I saw where the tracks of the horses went I'd be a little happier.

I'd gotten about ten feet when a whistling whine went by my right ear and then I heard the crack of what could only be a rifle. I didn't take any time to think about it—I just hit the ground, yanking my rifle out of its scabbard as I went.

There wasn't a speck of cover anywhere near me, and I felt just about as conspicuous as it's possible for a man to be. I looked around, trying to see where that shot had come from, but there was nothing but heat and dust and sage. If I didn't figure it out and do something about it, I was the next thing to dead.

Binny hadn't spooked, for a wonder, and I considered trying to get close enough to him to use him for cover until I could get to some rocks. Now that I looked more closely I could see that there was a little outcropping of them over behind the horse. As soon as I had the idea, he gave a little snort like he'd read my mind, and headed away from me at a brisk walk.

It seemed to me that those rocks would be the most likely place for whoever had been shooting at me to be holding up, so as soon as Binny was in a direct line between me and the rocks, I took my chance. I was on my feet and heading for the rocks as quickly as I've ever moved in my life, but it takes an awful lot of speed to outrun a bullet.

Luckily, I didn't have to. I made it to the rocks without another shot or anything else to show that I wasn't totally alone. I stood there with my back against one, getting my breath back and wondering what I should do.

It was a little bit of a shock to me when a voice suddenly said, "That you, Luke?"

"Clay? What the devil were you shooting at me for?" I gasped indignantly, spinning around to see where he was.

"I didn't notice it was you just at first," he said in a weak voice.

I didn't like the sound of that. Normally, I'd expect Clay to be able to recognize me about a half mile away. That made me think things were a long way from normal.

I walked in among the rocks, and there he was, propped up against one of them. He was drawn and white, and he had a bloody white handkerchief tied around his head. He looked terrible, but he was grinning.

"What are you smiling at?" I asked in surprise. "The herd's missing, the crew is gone, and you look like you've been shot."

"I'm alive," he pointed out. "And now that

you're here, it kind of looks like I might stay that way."

"It's a good thing you didn't hit me, then," I told him.

"Yeah," he admitted. "And it should have been a real easy shot." Then he passed out cold at my feet.

I knelt down beside him and felt for his pulse. It was there all right. It felt pretty strong and pretty steady to me, so I took off the makeshift bandage and took a closer look at his head. The bullet had cut a furrow along his scalp just over his left ear. It didn't look all that deep to me, but on the other hand he was unconscious. I didn't like that much. I went over to where Binny had started to graze, hoping he wouldn't take a notion to play hard to get. When I reached out for his bridle, he looked at me suspiciously and snorted a little, just like I hadn't been giving him oats and apples for years, but he held still until I had a good hold on him. I led him over nearer to Clay and tied him to a little bush, then took my canteen from the saddle and a clean handkerchief from one of the saddlebags.

I cleaned Clay's head as well as I was able, and while I was doing it, I tried to remember from the map we'd used as our guide how far ahead the next town was. It was a day's ride back to the last one, but unless there was another horse stashed around here somewhere, it was going to take a little longer than that. Binny could carry double some of the way, but the pace would be slower and I'd have to do some walking.

On the other hand the next town might be over the next ridge. I just didn't know. Clay could tell me, but he wasn't talking just now and I didn't know when he would be. I didn't know whether to start out in one direction or the other, or wait for Clay to come to.

He solved the problem for me by groaning and opening his eyes.

"I've got a headache," he muttered thickly.

"Not too surprising," I told him. "You want a drink?"

"Yeah. I've been wanting one since last night."

I held the canteen for him. "Is that when all this happened?"

"Uh-huh. They kind of took me by surprise."

"What about the others?"

"That's one of the things that surprised me," he said. "They were all in on it."

"All three of them?"

"Every one."

"How'd you get away?"

"I think they thought I was dead."

I nodded. "I suppose they could have. There's sure enough blood on you."

"They took all the horses too," he added, closing his eyes.

"Yeah," I muttered. "I noticed. Which reminds me, how far ahead is the next town?"

He opened his eyes and looked at me in a confused sort of way. "About half a day, I think."

"Then we'd better get going," I told him. "It's going to take a little longer than that with only one horse."

"I guess that means I've got to get up?"

"I guess so," I agreed, standing up and reaching down to give him a hand. "Just don't try to move too fast."

I pulled him to his feet, and he stood there swaying dizzily for a minute. "I don't suppose you'd like to wait a little while before we get started?" he asked.

"I'd rather not if you think you can make it. It's still early enough so we might make it before dark, and I'd kind of like to get another opinion on your head."

He rubbed the back of his hand against his forehead. "I'd settle for just another head," he told me. "Well, if you think we ought to go, let's do it. I have a feeling you're thinking straighter than I am just now."

It took two tries to get him into the saddle, and then I decided that I'd better ride too, at least for a while, or he'd never stay in the saddle. I mounted up behind him, and he sagged a little. "Darn," he muttered. "I don't feel much like I'm going to stay on here."

"Don't worry about it," I advised him. "I'm not about to let you fall off. Due east?"

"Due east," he agreed.

We rode along in silence for a few minutes. Clay was swaying a little, but he seemed to grow steadier as we went.

After a while he asked, "Did the herd come this way?"

"Nope. Or if they did, they were flying. There isn't a sign of a track."

"We might not get back this way for a day or so, Luke."

"You think I ought to look?"

"I guess so."

I turned Binny around and headed back toward the campsite. I ought to have thought of that myself, but the truth was that I was kind of anxious to get Clay to a doctor and it just hadn't crossed my mind. Clay was right, though. If there was a big storm or if another herd passed through here before we got back, we might never find out what direction our herd had taken. And one thing was certain— neither one of us was about to let that herd drift out of our lives.

I circled around the ground the herd had been bedded down in about a hundred yards out. Finally I cut the tracks they'd made as they were driven off.

"They headed south," I told Clay.

"Maybe we should follow them a way?"

"I don't think so. You don't look all that good to me. We'll head for that town, rest up a little, and get another horse. Then we'll see."

"Suits me, I guess. Just don't forget which way they went. I think I already have."

"Take it easy. I'll do the worrying for a while."

He took me at my word and concentrated on staying on the horse. I turned back in the direction we'd been going and wondered whether we'd ever see any of those cattle again. And, even more important, at least to me—the horses.

I'd sort of been keeping it out of my mind, but they had my three best horses, including Liz. That little mare wasn't quite as important to me as Clay, which was why we were heading for town instead of after the herd, but she came close. I'd been there when she was born, and we'd taken to each other right off. I'd never seen a horse quite like her before and I never expect to see one again. I was a long way from ready to write her off.

"Don't worry. We'll get her back," Clay said. He had a habit of reading my mind like that.

"By the way," he added, "how are *you* feeling?"

"I was feeling pretty good until I got back to camp," I said. "Now I sort of feel a relapse coming on."

"Serves you right," he said drowsily. "It was a silly thing to do."

Well, he was right about that. I certainly never intended to get measles again if I could help it. I'd started out as soon as I'd been able to, but now it looked like I'd been a little on the late side. I said as much to Clay.

"Not from where I'm sitting," he said. "If you'd gotten there much earlier, we might both be sitting back there in those rocks without a horse. Now, would you mind keeping it down a little? I'd sort of like to take a nap."

Chapter Five

That wasn't a real pleasant ride. Whenever Clay seemed awake enough to hold on for himself, I walked to let Binny take a breather, but that got to be less often as the day wore on. Which might have been just as well. I hadn't been out of bed all that long and I still wasn't in top shape.

It was just about dinnertime when we reached the outskirts of a little town with a signpost announcing it as Coldwater. The streets seemed pretty well deserted, but there was a towheaded little kid sitting on a rock just under the signpost, and he looked like he might be able to answer a few questions.

"You got a doctor in town, kid?"

"I reckon," he said. "Is that an outlaw, mister?"

No question, Clay wasn't looking like his usual self. "Nope. He had a run-in with a bunch of rustlers, though." I figured the kid would like that.

"Gosh, hadn't you better see the sheriff?"

"Got one of those too, huh? I guess I'll see him after I take my friend here to the doctor."

"I can show you where to find both of them," the kid told me. "Or I could show you where the doctor is and then go get the sheriff."

"Okay," I agreed.

"And then I could take your horse over to the livery stable. I could tell them to give him some grain and a rubdown and then—"

"Whoa. That sounds like plenty. Why don't you just lead the way to the doctor for a starter."

"Sure thing, mister."

He led the way down the street, asking me more questions about rustlers and outlaws than any ten men could have answered. He didn't seem particularly discouraged when I couldn't tell him what he wanted to know, and as soon as he'd pointed out the doctor's office door to me, he took off down the street after the sheriff.

I gave a knock on the doctor's door, and after a minute it was opened by a pleasant-looking middle-aged man. "If it's a hangover, it's too early and you ought to be ashamed of yourself," he told me in a tired voice. Then he looked past me to where Clay sat swaying in the saddle. "On the other hand," he went on, "if that friend of yours is in as rough shape as he looks, maybe you'd better stop fooling around out here and bring him on in."

I went over and managed to wake Clay up enough to get him out of the saddle.

"Are we there?" he mumbled as I helped him up the path.

"Yeah."

"Good. Where's there?"

"Never mind. There's a doctor here who's going to take a look at you."

"Seems like that might be a good idea," he admitted, trying to focus on me.

I eased him through the door and into a large paneled hallway with chairs lined up along the walls. Two of the chairs were occupied, and a little, skinny, mean-looking lady glared at us from one of them.

"I've been waiting for nearly an hour, Dr. Jenneckes," she said sharply. "I should think that a regular patient might get a little consideration around here, but I suppose that you're going to take that drifter in ahead of people that have been sitting here for heaven—"

"Now, Miss Snithel," the doctor said cheerfully, "you know the rules of Hippocrates, which I'm obliged to follow: People who've been kicked, stabbed, shot, or poisoned come first."

She sniffed. "Also small boys, pretty girls, and drunken cowhands."

"See, you do know the rules," he told her, opening a door at the end of a short hallway. "Bring him in here," he told me.

We stepped through into the doctor's office, and I sat Clay down on his examining table.

"You can wait in the hall or stay in here," the doctor told me.

"Thanks. I don't figure it's too safe to get anywhere near that Miss Snithel."

"Then grab a seat and tell me what happened."

"Well, first off," I said, as he started looking at Clay's head, "I'm Luke Johnson and that's my partner, Clay Peters. He's been shot."

"I could tell."

"Yeah, I guess so. Anyway, we own a ranch in Braxton. We were driving about eight hundred head of cattle to the railroad. I got measles and had to sit things out for a few days. When I caught up, the cattle were gone, the crew was gone, and Clay was in pretty much the shape you see now. How is he?"

"Could be a lot worse," Dr. Jenneckes said. He was dabbing at the wound with some kind of red stuff and Clay looked like it was waking him up a little. "It's pretty much of a giant-sized scratch."

"That's what I thought," I said, "but he keeps falling asleep."

"He's probably tired. It isn't very restful, getting shot. He'll be all right in a day or two."

"Good," I said, feeling a lot better. "I was getting a little nervous."

"We haven't really got a day or two to waste," Clay said suddenly. He hadn't looked like he was paying any attention.

"They aren't going to be moving all that fast with eight hundred head of cattle, Clay. We can manage a day or two."

The door of the office burst open and there was my towheaded kid again.

"The sheriff won't come," he told me breathlessly. "He says he's sick of my stories and I should just get home to supper before my ma gives me a hiding. I figured I'd better come back and tell you first, though."

I kept from grinning and nodded gravely. "Thanks a lot, partner," I told him. "I'll be sure to tell the sheriff how much help you've been."

"Gee, thanks, mister. Hope you get those rustlers."

"Nice kid," the doctor commented, "but his imagination's a little overactive."

"Yeah," I said with a grin. "I guess I can find the sheriff on my own."

The doctor had finished cleaning Clay's head and was now putting on a neat white bandage. "Now then, my friend," he said to Clay, "I want you to take it easy for two days at least. That means you get plenty of sleep, you get plenty to eat, and you don't do any riding around. Is that clear?"

"Sure," Clay said. "That sounds like a pretty good idea to me."

"Do it whether it sounds like a good idea or not. You'll probably have quite a headache for a while. If it starts getting a lot worse or if you start seeing double, you come on back."

I had a feeling he was talking more to me than to Clay.

"You wouldn't know of a good place for us to stay, would you?" I asked.

"They have a couple of rooms over the saloon," he said. "It gets pretty noisy on Saturday night, but I imagine you'll be gone by then."

I paid him and thanked him, and was given a little bottle of laudanum syrup for Clay in case he couldn't sleep, and also strict instructions not to use it for more than two nights in a row.

"Well," I said after we made it past the cranky woman in the waiting room, "you look a little better than you did when we went in there."

"I just wish I felt better," Clay told me.

"What I'd like right now is a bath. A nice hot one that I could soak in for about an hour and someone to keep adding hot water."

I smiled at him. "If we can find a bathtub, I'll take care of the hot water, but I don't know how good our chances are. And shouldn't I see the sheriff first?"

"Maybe," he said. "Although it seems to me that if he were any good, he would have listened to what that kid had to say and checked on it before he sent him home."

I considered that. Clay had been the sheriff in Braxton for a year or so, and if he said that the sheriff should have listened, then he was probably right. Clay had been a pretty good sheriff.

"I guess, then," I said, "I'll wait till after dinner for the sheriff."

We found the saloon without any trouble. It was the only building with two stories on Main Street. We walked through the doors and stood looking around the empty room.

"Kind of empty," I said. Raising my voice, I called, "Anybody here?"

The words echoed around the room, but there was no answer. Then, just as I was about to call again, I heard an odd sound coming from the back of the building. I couldn't tell what it was, and I looked over at Clay to see if he knew. He shrugged, then winced. The major part of the sound was an odd sort of panting with a funny kind of shuffling noise at regular intervals.

It grew louder, and suddenly the door at the back of the room near the bar was thrust open. Through it we could see what had to be the fattest man in the world. For a minute I couldn't imagine how he planned to get through that doorway, but then he turned sideways and with a repetition of that shuffling noise he eased his bulk through.

"Howdy, gents," he said in a high, wheezy voice that pretty well accounted for the panting sound. "What can I do for you?"

I wondered if he could fit behind the bar, and considered asking for a beer just to find out.

"Dr. Jenneckes told us you might have a couple of rooms we could rent for a night or two," I said.

"That's right. Two real nice rooms upstairs. They've got windows and everything. Two bits a night and that includes a lock on the door."

"Fine," I said. "We'll take 'em. You wouldn't have a bathtub, would you?"

"Yes, sir, I would. All the conveniences in this establishment. You want a nice hot bath, and that's what you're going to get. I'll start the boy heating the water. He'll bring it up shortly."

He waddled over to the bar and grabbed a

couple of keys. "Here you are, boys," he said, holding them out. "Rooms are up at the top of the stairs on the right. You can get dinner just down the street at the Cold Springs Café. It'll be open for another hour."

I took the keys and thanked him. We started up the stairs, and I was glad that he hadn't felt it necessary to show us to our rooms. I didn't think the stairs would support him for more than a second.

I gave Clay a hand after the third step, but he still looked pretty tired before we reached the top. I opened the door to the first room, and he went right in and collapsed on the bed.

"I think I'd better bring you your dinner," I told him. "I've got a notion you don't want to go up and down those stairs again."

"You're right," he told me, closing his eyes. "The only thing that's getting me off this bed is that bathtub."

"What do you want to eat?"

"Whatever you have, but only half as much."

"I'm cutting down," I told him. "A man could end up like that guy downstairs."

"Does that mean you'll have only one piece of pie for dessert?" he asked me skeptically, opening one eye.

"Actually, I was thinking of having only one biscuit with my chicken."

The café was a tiny place with a grimy window in the door and all of the best sorts of smells coming out as soon as I opened it. I went right in and sat down at the only empty table in the place, and before I was much more than settled in the chair a tired-looking waitress was there to take my order.

"What'll it be?" she asked, not sounding all that interested.

"Whatever's smelling so good."

"Everything smells good. You want to narrow it down a little, mister?"

"Chicken pie, then, with everything. And when I'm done, I'd like to take some back to the saloon for a sick friend."

"Sure thing. You got to bring the plates back in the morning, though, or the cook will come looking for them."

"Don't worry," I told her. "I don't want any cooks mad at me. They're too mean."

That almost got a smile from her.

While I was waiting for my chicken pie, I scanned every face in the room. It didn't seem too likely that any of the hands whom Clay had hired for the herd would be here. I imagined that they were heading south with all those cattle. On the other hand, it wouldn't hurt to check.

I didn't see any familiar faces. Of course, I'd

seen those three only once, briefly, but I thought I might recognize them again.

Then I realized that one of the men I was looking at was wearing a badge. This seemed like a good chance to kill two birds with one stone, so I stood up and walked over toward his table.

"Sheriff?"

He looked up from his dinner, a tall man with just the beginning of a bald spot and a potbelly.

"What can I do for you, mister?"

"My partner and I ran into a little trouble about a half-day's ride to the west. A kid might have mentioned it to you a little earlier. I thought maybe I ought to talk to you about it."

"To the west, huh? I'm not sure that would be in my jurisdiction."

That kind of irritated me. "Are you sure it isn't?"

He looked at me thoughtfully. "Suppose you tell me what happened?"

I gave him the story without any frills, and he nodded when I'd finished. "Sounds like a bunch that's been operating in this area for a while. I'd say you two were lucky. Usually there isn't anyone left alive to make a complaint."

"Well, this time there is. What are you planning to do about it?"

"Nothing I can do. Even if it had happened in my jurisdiction, they sure aren't in it now."

"You got any suggestions, then?"

"You might try to get hold of a Federal marshal, I suppose."

"Oh, sure," I said. "Of course, by that time the whole herd would be hamburger."

"Sorry, mister, my hands are tied."

"Yeah," I said. I got up and headed back to my own table. My timing was good on that, at least. The waitress was standing there with a steaming plate of chicken pie.

"If that tastes as good as it smells, I'll have to ask your cook to marry me."

"He's already married," she said with a sniff.

By the time I got to dessert I'd long since forgotten that I'd been planning to cut down, and I had two pieces of the best custard pie I'd ever eaten. Then I settled back with a cup of coffee to wait for Clay's dinner.

While I sat I tried to do a little planning. Once Clay was ready to travel we'd probably be able to pick up the track of the herd without too much trouble. Eight hundred cattle leave a pretty big trail. The question was what we were supposed to do once we caught up with them. There were only two of us and at least four of them from what Clay had said. From what the sheriff had said, there were probably even more than that. We might get lucky but it wasn't something we ought to count on.

Of course, we might find the law more cooperative when we caught up with them. There couldn't be all that many sheriffs like this one. I'd look around for a horse for Clay tomorrow and see if I could pick up any more information about the gang around town than the sheriff had been willing to part with. Maybe, by the time we were ready to leave, we'd have some kind of plan worked out. That idea cheered me up a little, and I collected Clay's supper and went back to the room all set to talk the whole thing over with him.

The saloon was nearly as empty as it had been when we first got there, with just two cowpunchers leaning against the bar and not seeming to have much to say.

I went up the stairs and into Clay's room, wondering what he'd think about the sheriff's attitude. Then I decided that maybe I'd wait until morning to ask him.

He'd finished his bath and the tub of water was cooling in front of the window. After that, I guess he'd just piled right into bed and gone straight to sleep.

Too bad I'd drunk that second cup of coffee. It looked sort of like I'd have to eat his dinner.

Chapter Six

It was about eight o'clock the next morning when I looked around the door of Clay's room and saw that he was awake.

"How are you feeling?"

"Like someone shot me," he said, pulling himself up to a sitting position. "I guess I fell asleep last night before you got back. Did you talk to the sheriff?"

"Yeah," I said, walking into the room. "Seems like nothing that happened or that might happen is ever going to happen in his jurisdiction."

"That's not going to be too much help to us."

"Nope. I thought I might ask around town a little, though. The sheriff seemed to think this might be a gang that's operated around here before. If so, maybe somebody will have some idea of where we ought to look for them."

Clay nodded. "Could be. I think we ought to get some breakfast."

"Do you want me to bring you some?"

"No, thanks. I'd like to get a little fresh air."

"Okay. I'll go and check on Binny while you get dressed. Better wait until I get back to try those stairs."

"Don't take all day. I'm hungry."

I'd intended to ask about buying another horse when I'd taken Binny to the livery stable the night before, but the owner hadn't been there. The kid who was watching the place hadn't known whether any of the horses were for sale.

As I walked up to the place a shrewd-looking man, maybe sixty years old, who reminded me a lot of my Uncle Jack, came out the door.

"Can I help you, mister?" he asked.

"I left my horse here last night," I told him. "Just thought I'd check on him."

He nodded. "Nice-looking horse." He stood aside and let me go ahead of him into the stable.

"You got any horses for sale?" I asked him.

"Might have. Not as good as that one, of course."

"That's all right. I couldn't afford one as good as that one."

He didn't comment on that, just looked thoughtful.

We walked over to Binny's stall, and he nickered a greeting.

"Well, you don't look any the worse for wear," I told him. "I guess you're the only one."

"You wouldn't be the fellas whose herd got stolen, would you?" the stable owner asked.

"That's right. I wasn't with the herd at the time, but my partner wasn't quite so lucky."

"Is he okay?"

"Got a headache. The doctor said he'd be all right in a day or two. That's why I need the horse."

"I've got a couple out in the corral you might want to take a look at."

I nodded. "I'll bring him over after breakfast," I said. "Do you know anything about these rustlers? The sheriff seemed to think they'd been operating around here for a while."

He nodded. "Not that anybody knows much, you understand. But we've found a few camps with a lot of bodies and no cattle. Did the rest of your crew get killed?"

"Nope. As far as we can tell, the rest of our crew were all rustlers."

He looked surprised, so I explained to him what had happened.

"So the two of you can identify at least some of the rustlers, then?"

"Yeah. I guess they figured that Clay was dead and the rest of us were just hands hired on for the drive. We didn't get much of a look at them, anyway."

"They probably figured they were safe enough," he agreed. "Well, you bring that partner of yours over, and we'll see if we can find a horse to suit him."

When I got back to the room, Clay was more than ready for breakfast and a little bit irritated that I'd taken so long.

"I didn't get two dinners last night," he pointed out. "I didn't even get one. Somebody ate it."

"I suppose you wanted me to wake you up?"

"What I want is to get some breakfast."

"Then quit complaining and let's go."

When we got to the top of the stairs he looked at them a little doubtfully. "Pretty steep," he commented.

"Are you sure you don't want me to bring you something?"

"I'm sure," he said. "You go first. If I slip, you can break my fall."

"How about if I just take your arm to start with?" I said. "Otherwise I might end up breaking your fall with my neck."

By the time we got to the café Clay seemed a little shaky, but I had a feeling he'd rather I didn't comment on it, so I kept my mouth shut. We ordered some bacon and eggs with a lot of coffee and biscuits, and Clay managed to put away about half of his share before he ran out of steam.

"I guess you might as well have the rest of this," he told me. "It'll save you from ordering more."

"Okay," I said. "I talked to the owner of the livery stable about the rustlers. It sounds like we were pretty lucky."

"How do you mean?"

"We're both alive. That's the first time anyone's managed that with this lot."

He nodded. "Now all we have to do is figure out how to get that herd back. And the horses."

"We should be able to track them."

"Unless they hit a trail where there've been other herds. And even if we do find them, there's only two of us. Sometimes the law isn't all that much help."

"So what do you suggest?"

He shrugged. "I guess we just look until we find 'em, and then hope we can find some help."

"That sounds a lot like what I had in mind."

"We'll start tomorrow," he said.

"Not unless you feel a whole lot better than you do today."

"Don't worry. I will. In the meantime we'd better find me a horse."

"Now?"

"Sure, now. You got something better to do?"

"I guess not. Just let me finish this biscuit."

I finished my breakfast, and Clay had another cup of coffee while he waited for me. He was starting to look a little better by the time we'd paid the waitress.

Back at the livery stable it didn't take too long to see that only one of the horses for sale was going to be any good to us.

"I don't know," Clay said a little doubtfully. "It's a pinto. I've never had a pinto before."

"You've got a choice, Clay: You can have a pinto or a swayback. Which'll it be?"

"Since you put it that way. . . ."

We haggled for that horse for maybe half an hour, and by the end of that time I knew why the man reminded me of Uncle Jack. They were both sneaky, untruthful, devious, and just plain crooked when it came to horse-trading. I was glad I'd had the practice with my uncle, or we wouldn't have come out of it with whole skins.

"How's our money holding out?" Clay asked as we left the livery stable.

"Pretty well," I said. "I won a little on a horse race back in Sanford Junction. If we don't have to follow 'em too far, we ought to do okay."

"It occurs to me that I'm going to need a

saddle and bridle too. Also a bedroll and maybe some saddlebags."

"I suppose they took all the money you were carrying?"

"That's right. Unless. . . ."

He stopped and reached down into the top of his boot. He fumbled for a minute and then pulled out a twenty-dollar gold piece.

"They didn't get that," he said happily.

"You got a pocket in there or something?" I asked.

"Yeah. I haven't even thought about it for the last year or two. I've been carrying this gold piece around since the war."

"Well, let's hope we don't need it," I said, "but it's nice to know it's there. You want to go to look for a saddle now?"

He hesitated, then said, "I'm getting a little tired. Could you take care of it?"

"I don't see why not. Do you want some help with those stairs, first?"

He shook his head. "I'm a little steadier on my feet than I was earlier. I don't think I'll have any trouble. Maybe I'll stop in the bar and see if the barkeep has any more information about that bunch of rustlers. See you later, Luke."

I got the saddle and bridle and such that Clay needed, then added a few supplies for the trail. It put a pretty fair dent in our money since we didn't have so much as a coffeepot or a can opener, never mind any coffee or cans to open, but once we were out on the trail we wouldn't need too much cash, I figured.

By the time I got back to the hotel, Clay was asleep again. I thought about it and decided there wasn't a lot I could do before lunchtime, so I went downstairs and had that kid start heating up bathwater again. There was no reason for Clay to be the only clean one.

Chapter Seven

"Wake up, Luke. It's time to get started."

I opened my eyes reluctantly to the gray early-morning light of the room and squinted up at Clay. "It's not even light out yet," I protested.

"It will be by the time you get up," he told me. "Get a move on."

"I guess there's no need to ask if you're feeling better this morning," I said, sitting up and swinging my feet over the edge of the bed.

"Quit stalling, Luke. I've got the horses saddled, and I've ordered breakfast at the café. I'll see you there."

He left and I got up and splashed some water in my face. Some mornings it's easier to wake up than others. It didn't take me too long to get dressed, but I had quite a time getting a straight part in my hair. It kept trying to dodge off toward the right.

63

Clay was halfway through his breakfast by the time I joined him.

"I was just getting ready to come wake you up again," he told me.

"Took a while to get everything straightened out," I said vaguely.

"So I see," he said, looking at my hair. Clay never misses much.

I didn't bother to answer him, just started eating.

"Luke, when you were buying supplies yesterday, did you happen to think of a pistol for me?"

I looked at him in surprise. "Now that you mention it, no."

"I've got the rifle, but that's it."

"Darn. We're getting a little short, but I think you've got to have one."

"There goes the twenty-dollar gold piece," Clay said glumly.

"And the early start," I added.

We got the revolver and some ammunition for it, and then we headed out of town. Now that we both had horses it took us only four hours to get back to where the herd had been attacked. The tracks were still nice and clear.

"I wonder why they went south," Clay said. "Where could they sell them down that way any quicker than if they headed southeast to the railhead?"

"Might just be to throw off anyone trying to follow them."

"Maybe, but chances are they didn't expect there'd be anyone interested in following."

"Well, there's only one way I can think of to find out."

"Right," he agreed, and gave his horse a little kick.

We followed those tracks all morning, riding at a good, fast pace, not enough to really tire the horses but enough to make up for some lost time so it wouldn't take too many days to catch up with the herd. I was keeping my eyes open for horses' hoofprints too. For one thing, I wanted to get an idea of how many men there were with the herd. For another, I was looking for Liz's prints. Every once in a while I'd see a track where she'd tried to break away from the remuda.

"Hold on a minute, Clay," I called out at one point.

He pulled up and came over to where I was staring down at the ground.

"Liz," he said, looking down.

"Yeah. I want to see how far she got. She might have broken loose."

He nodded. "You follow. I'll ride along the main track and see if I can spot her getting driven back in."

It wasn't easy to follow the trail once I was

clear of the beaten-down track, but finally I saw where she'd started to veer back toward the herd. It looked like one of the rustlers had been riding farther back than the remuda and had managed to cut her off.

I turned and headed back toward the trail. In a minute I joined Clay where he was bending over some marks on the ground.

"This is where she got back to the herd," he said as I rode up. "Looks to me like they hobbled her."

"The dirty skunks."

"Guess they figured they might not be lucky enough to catch her next time."

"They were right about that, anyway," I said.

We followed the tracks for the next two days. The air was hot and humid, and I kept expecting a thunderstorm to come up and wipe out the trail. I kept a close eye on Clay, but he seemed to be all right. No matter how tired he got, he always felt better after we'd rested awhile.

We were getting closer to that herd all the time, but they'd started to move faster too, and we were still a little better than a day behind when I noticed something different.

"I think maybe there aren't quite as many of them," I said.

"Of what, Luke?"

"Anything. Seems like the herd is smaller and the remuda tracks don't seem . . . in fact, I haven't seen any of Liz's prints in a while."

"What do you think is going on?"

"They're breaking up the herd," I guessed.

"So what do we do now?"

"I think we'd better find out where they cut off from the rest of the herd and what direction they were moving in. I can't understand why we didn't notice."

"That's easy," Clay said. "We're getting sloppy. We haven't been watching the edges. We've been riding right down the middle. With a trail this easy to follow, we just stopped paying close attention."

"All right, then, let's go."

It took us about an hour to get back to where part of the herd had split off from the rest. Now that we were looking for it, it was pretty easy to spot.

"Who do we follow?" Clay asked.

Before I could answer there was a distant crash of thunder. I looked over toward the west and saw the tallest thunderhead you could imagine, and it was heading toward us.

Clay said, "I hope there isn't any hail in that thing, or we're liable to get our brains beaten out. Do you see anything we could use for cover?"

"Not a thing," I told him. "And I don't think

we're going to have much time to do any look-ing," I added as a violent wind sprang up.

The thunderhead was moving toward us with incredible speed, and Clay looked at it again and then swung off his horse.

"We'd better get flat," he said, "or we're lia-ble to end up human lightning rods."

I couldn't argue with that, so I joined him on the ground and then got Binny off his feet. Clay looked at his pinto doubtfully, wondering, I guess, whether he'd have to throw him. He didn't need to give it a thought. That horse took one look at Binny lying there on the ground and lay right down beside him.

"And you didn't want a pinto," I said, shak-ing my head. "Now us," I added, lying down with part of my weight across Binny's neck. I didn't want him getting scared and deciding to jump up.

"When you were buying things I wish you'd thought of slickers," Clay muttered.

"Me too, but I thought beans were more im-portant."

Clay started to say something else, but what-ever it was, was drowned out in a sudden flash of lightning and crack of thunder right over our heads. Before my ears stopped ringing, the rain sheeted down like someone had opened a set of floodgates.

Rain isn't very often warm at the best of

times, but I've never felt it as cold as that before or since. I was soaked through in a minute and immediately I was shaking like a leaf. The temperature of the air must have dropped thirty degrees in no time at all.

As if that wasn't enough, I felt something hit me a stinging blow on the shoulder and realized that Clay's wish wasn't going to be granted. There was hail, all right. I wrapped my arms around my head and wriggled around so that I was covering what I could of Binny's head as well. I just hoped that there wasn't too much of it. I'd seen more than one cow battered to death in one of these sudden hailstorms.

We were lucky. As hail went, it wasn't too big or too bad. On the other hand, it wasn't any picnic. I realized pretty soon that unless it got worse it wasn't likely to kill us, but I felt like a dozen small boys were throwing all their marbles at me all at once.

After what seemed like hours the hail started to taper off, but the rain went on and on.

Finally Clay said, "Are you all right, Luke?"

"Aside from being wet, cold, and miserable, you mean?"

"Yeah."

"Fine, I guess. Do you think the lightning's stopped?"

"Haven't noticed any in a while. Does it seem like it's getting dark to you?"

"Kind of. I don't know whether it's the clouds getting thicker or sundown."

"I'm getting up now," he said with sudden decision. "I think I might just drown if I don't."

We both got to our feet, then stood back to let the horses up.

Clay stretched stiffly. "I feel like someone's been pounding on me for a couple of hours. Is that sound your teeth chattering, or is there a rattler dumb enough to be out in this weather?"

"It's my teeth," I told him. "Do you suppose there's anything within a day's ride of here that's dry enough to burn?"

"Just my mouth," he said. "Got any suggestions?"

"I think we'd better head in the direction that piece of the herd was going."

"Why?"

"I figure they were going someplace special and not too far away. They must have had a market for those cattle right near here."

"Probably just wishful thinking," Clay said. "On the other hand, I haven't got any better ideas. Let's go before we freeze to death."

So we went. Clay remembered which direction to take. I'd gotten a little turned around in the storm and wouldn't have been sure.

We rode for hours, or anyway that's how it seemed to me, and I was starting to think that we might go on forever when somewhere ahead in the darkness I saw a gleam of light.

"You see that, Clay?" I asked.

"Looks like a light, doesn't it?"

"It does to me," I agreed, "but I could just be getting light-headed."

"Let's go find out," he suggested, urging his horse into a tired trot.

As we rode ahead into the continuing rain, the light got brighter and was joined by one or two dimmer ones.

"I think that must be a town," I said. "They might even have a place with a fire there somewhere."

"I'd settle for a place to put on some dry clothes and enough of a roof to keep them that way," Clay told me.

A few minutes later we were there, wherever there was. By this time it was so dark that we couldn't see anything except the light shining through a few windows.

"I think that might be a saloon," Clay said, pointing down the street.

"I guess a drink would do just about as well as a fire," I conceded.

We rode down to the building that seemed to have a few more lights than any of the others. Sure enough, Clay had been right. We swung down off the horses and tied them to the rack in front.

"Don't worry, fellas," I told them. "We'll find out where the stables are and come back to you."

I pushed in through the doors and stood there blinking in the sudden light. It seemed like there was some sort of organ music off to one side of the room, and as I turned my head to look, there was a sudden commotion on the other side.

"Look out, Luke!" Clay said suddenly, and shoved me to the side. I grabbed for my gun as I fell, figuring that it had to be that kind of problem, and heard the boom of a .45 from just above my head. I hit the floor rolling and stopped on my belly with my Colt pointed across the room. In another few seconds, sprawled on the floor with a splotch of blood in the center of his chest was one of the men I'd seen that day when Clay brought the new crew out to the camp. I rose slowly to my feet, gun still in hand, and scanned the rest of the room. Behind me, I knew that Clay would be doing the same.

"Is that the only one?" I asked him.

"It's the only one of the three I hired, anyway," he said. "We don't know what the others look like."

Before I could answer, a door at the back of the saloon opened and the biggest and hairiest man I've ever seen walked in. He had a gun in his hand and a star on his chest, and I had a feeling he didn't get too many arguments.

"All right, gentlemen," he said in a cool voice, "perhaps you'd like to explain just what's going on here?"

I was about to try when suddenly two hands clamped around my wrists from behind, and I realized that even if I'd wanted to, I couldn't have moved a muscle in my hand. Which meant that I wasn't very likely to be firing the gun I was holding.

I looked around at Clay and saw that he hadn't been taken quite so much by surprise. Only one of his wrists had been grabbed, and he had the grabber stalemated with a gun pointing right at the middle of her face.

I looked around enough to see that I was also being held by a girl. She couldn't have been more than sixteen, and she looked enough like the other one to be her twin sister.

Clay blinked and lowered his gun. "Excuse me, miss," he said.

"That's perfectly all right," she replied with a shy smile. "You're under arrest."

Chapter Eight

The man with the badge stepped forward. "I'm supposed to say that, Susie. Now suppose you two just put your guns down and your hands up."

That seemed like a sensible idea to me. The only problem was that the girl still had a hold on my wrists.

"Uh, miss, I'd be glad to put the gun down if you'd let go."

"Oh," she said. "Of course. We don't do this very often. I'm not used to it."

She let me go, and I put the gun down on the floor. Clay did the same, and now we both turned back to the sheriff.

"Would it do any good to point out that he drew first?" Clay asked.

"That depends on how many other people say so," the sheriff told him. As he strode through the room, I noticed that everyone in the place stayed out of his line of fire.

"What happened to you two?" he asked when he reached us. "Your hands are black and blue."

"Hailstorm," I told him. Now that the excitement was dying down I was starting to feel cold and wet and sore again.

"I don't suppose you'd like to ask these people what they saw?" Clay asked patiently.

"In due course," the sheriff said. "First, I think, we'll get the two of you over to the jail. Anyone who thinks he knows what happened can come along," he added, raising his voice enough so that everyone in the room could hear.

"Susie, Sally, you two better get home. Your mama's going to be wondering what happened to you."

"All right, Pa," the one behind me said. "Will you be home for dinner?"

"Can't be sure, honey. Tell your mama to keep some warm."

I blinked. "Are they your daughters or your deputies, sheriff?" I asked as they left the saloon.

"Both, mister. Now suppose the two of you just walk right on across that street."

We went back out into the rain. I'd thought I was as wet as I could get, but somehow I seemed to be even wetter by the time we went into the sheriff's office.

"Now then," the sheriff said, "you two just sit down right over there against the wall and tell me what happened. After that, Charlie and Pete can tell me if that's the way they saw it."

Charlie and Pete were the only two men who'd followed us over from the saloon. One of them was a skinny old codger who looked maybe a hundred years old. He had a funny little beard and sparse white hair, and his little black eyes looked like they could see through a brick wall.

The other man was maybe thirty-five and was the closest thing to a normal-looking person we'd seen yet in this town.

"All right," the sheriff said. "Start talking."

"Look," said Clay, who looked a little tired under the mud on his face, "this is kind of a long story, and we're wet and cold. Could we maybe change into something dry first?"

That seemed like a good idea to me, but the sheriff looked a little undecided.

"Let 'em, Don," the younger man suggested. "The other guy really did shoot first. Pete here can tell you about it, and I'll go get the ring—the mayor—while they're changing."

"All right, Charlie," the sheriff said. "But I guess if they're going to get out of those wet clothes, they'll probably want their saddlebags."

"We'd appreciate it," I said with chattering teeth.

Charlie nodded and stepped out into the night.

"What about it, Pete?" the sheriff asked. "What happened?"

"The door opened. These two came in. The dead fella pulled a gun." He pointed at Clay. "That fella shot him."

Well, that was short and to the point.

"That seems clear enough," the sheriff said, turning back to us. "As soon as Charlie gets back with the mayor, maybe you can tell us why."

The door of the office opened and Charlie tossed in our saddlebags. "Here you go," he said. "Be right back."

I bent painfully to pick up my bag and opened the buckle with stiff fingers. I'd kept those saddlebags well oiled, and all my clothes were still dry. I pulled out a shirt and looked over at Clay.

"Your stuff get wet?"

"The shirt did," he said disgustedly.

"Take one of mine," I told him, tossing over an extra. I unbuttoned my shirt and pulled it off, then reached for the dry one.

As I turned my back toward him, old Pete whistled in amazement. "That must have been some storm. You're black and blue all over your back, mister."

"Somehow that doesn't surprise me a lot," I said. "Offhand, I can't think of when I've had a more miserable afternoon."

"You can say that again," Clay muttered as we finished changing. "I don't think I'll ever be warm again."

"That wouldn't be coffee in that pot, would it?" I asked, deciding that Pete's story might have cleared us enough for a cup.

The sheriff looked over in surprise at the old potbellied stove in the corner. "I guess it would," he admitted. "That must have been what the girls were doing here. Their ma sent it over with them, and they just naturally had to come see what I was doing."

He went over and rummaged in a box on the floor until he came up with four battered tin mugs. "What about it, Pete? You want some too?"

"No."

I guessed that Pete was a man of few words.

The sheriff filled three of the mugs and handed one to each of us. I just sat and held it in my hands for a few minutes, trying to get some feeling back into them.

"Are you all right, Luke?" Clay asked me suddenly.

"Huh?"

"You're sort of swaying," he pointed out.

"Yeah, I'm fine. How about you? You're gray."

"That's mud," he explained, taking a swallow of his coffee.

"I guess we're both wrecks, then," I muttered.

The door of the office opened and Charlie came in. "The mayor had company for dinner, Don," he said. "He wants to know if this can wait till morning. Says hold 'em here overnight if you think you ought to. Otherwise, tell 'em to come back tomorrow."

The sheriff didn't look happy about it, but he nodded. "I hate to let 'em go, but if you both say the other fellow is the one who started things, I guess I can't really hold 'em." He looked over at us thoughtfully.

"Never mind, sheriff," Clay said. "This town doesn't look like it has a hotel."

"That's right."

"We'd be glad to stay right here, then. This isn't a night I want to spend sleeping out. We've gotten wet enough for one day. Is there any chance that we could get some dinner?"

"I guess that could be arranged," the sheriff said. "Charlie, would you mind asking my wife for a few extra helpings of stew for these two while I get the cell ready?"

"Sure thing, Don," Charlie said agreeably. "Be back in a few minutes."

By the time Charlie was back with two big plates of stew, some biscuits, and what looked like an apple pie, the sheriff had us in a cell in back of the office area. There was a stove in there too, and the sheriff had gotten it lit and given each of us a pillow and an extra blanket. He'd also sent Pete home, suggesting that he stop at the livery stable and send a boy over for our horses.

I looked at the food and at the bunk, and wondered if I was too tired to eat or too hungry to sleep.

Clay was digging into the food, so I sat on the bunk with my plate and took a forkful. That settled it. It might have been the best stew in the world but I couldn't even taste it.

"Here, Clay," I said. "You might as well have this too." I put it on the floor next to the bunk and crawled under the covers. I think I was asleep before Clay finished asking what was wrong with me.

The sun was flooding in through the bars of the window the next morning when I woke up. Clay was sitting there eating just like when I went to sleep, and for one confused minute I thought no time at all had passed. Then I noticed that it was flapjacks and sausage instead of stew. Whatever I'd felt like last night, I was plenty hungry now.

"Is there some of that for me?" I asked him, sitting up.

"Plenty," he said. "I guess Mrs. Morton figures everyone eats like her husband."

I looked around and saw another plate on a stool by the bars. Sure enough, it looked like there might even be a little bit more than I could eat.

"I take it that the sheriff's name is Morton," I said, cutting a healthy bite of the flapjacks.

"That's right. He's got some coffee out there too, if you're ready for it."

"I'm ready all right, but what I'd really like to see is the mayor. Now that I've dried out some, I want to see if there's anything left of that trail we were following."

"Not much chance of that," Clay said glumly. "Our best hope is that someone here in town saw them and knows where they were headed. For sure, as soon as they found out we shot Jeff over in the saloon, they took off."

"Yeah," I agreed, "but it's not too likely that they took anyone here into their confidence."

We finished eating, and the sheriff brought in more coffee. Then he let us out of the cell and escorted us back into the front office.

"The mayor ought to be here shortly. Charlie went to fetch him."

Sure enough, in a few minutes Charlie came in, followed by a man who I supposed was the mayor of this town. He was a tall, dark man with a curling black mustache, and he was wearing an honest-to-goodness black cape. That was surprising enough, but when he whipped it off and hung it on a peg by the door, I saw that it had a red-satin lining.

"Well, Don, what's going on here? Charlie says these two killed a man over in The Blue Door."

"That's right, Mr. Hawk. Charlie and Pete both say that the dead man drew first. I was just about to ask these two what it's all about."

"That sounds like a good idea to me," Mayor Hawk said. "Why don't we start with who they are and what they're doing here."

Clay looked at me, and I shrugged. Clay gets through a story faster than I do, and as far as I was concerned he could do all the talking.

"My name is Clay Peters," he told them. "This is my partner, Luke Johnson. We own a cattle and horse ranch in Braxton."

The mayor nodded. "That's about a hundred and fifty miles from here, isn't it? How did you end up shooting a man in our saloon?"

Clay started right off from the beginning of the drive and gave them the whole story straight through.

"Well, Mr. Peters," the mayor said when he

was finished, "I don't know that I like the sound of that at all. In fact, I'm a little bit at a loss. There is a herd such as you describe in town, but I see no reason to believe your story instead of Mr. Lee's."

"Mr. Lee?"

"The man who owns—the man who *says* he owns the herd. He arrived here yesterday morning. It seems that he'd heard we are interested in buying some beef. Since he had a few cattle, he thought he could make a deal with us. The terms were satisfactory, so—"

"You mean he sold you the herd?" Clay broke in tensely. "He's gone?"

"Not quite," the mayor said a little coolly. "We have a deal, as I said, but nothing's changed hands and they haven't left yet."

Clay settled back, looking relieved. "Well," he said, "it'll take a little time, of course, but our story can certainly be checked. The brand is ours, it's registered, and there shouldn't be any problem at all documenting the fact that we own those cattle."

"I suppose that's true," the mayor said. "You certainly don't seem to be worried about the outcome of an investigation. I suspect that the next thing for us to do is to go and have a talk with Mr. Lee. I imagine that if what you say is true, you'd just as soon he didn't have a chance to leave town. And I also imagine that even if he doesn't know who shot his man last night, it might make him a little nervous. I'd guess that the sooner we see him, the better it will be."

Chapter Nine

We rode out to the east of town with Mayor Hawk, the sheriff, and Charlie. The herd had been grazing on a piece of open range there while negotiations were taking place.

When we got there, Clay took one look around and nodded. "C Bar L. That's us. You say that no money has changed hands?"

"That's right," the mayor said.

"I think we ought to have a little talk with Mr. Lee," I said. "There's only about two hundred head here. I'd like to know where the rest of the herd was heading. And I'd like to know where the horses are."

"The camp is just over that rise," the sheriff said, giving his horse a little nudge.

"Do you think he has Liz with him?" Clay asked me as we followed the sheriff.

"I didn't see her tracks once after this bunch turned off," I told him. I reached down and loosened my rifle in its scabbard.

"This isn't supposed to be a shooting party, Johnson," the sheriff said, noticing my rifle.

"I won't start anything, sheriff," I promised. "I just want to be ready in case anyone else does."

We topped the rise and looked down on the camp. There was a chuck wagon and the remains of a campfire and that was all. Not one man, not one bedroll, and not one horse.

We stared down in silence for a minute.

"They must have heard about the shooting last night," Clay finally said. From his tone of voice most people would have figured he couldn't care less, but I knew better.

"I'd take this to mean that your story is true," the mayor said thoughtfully. "At least they left the cattle."

"They didn't leave the horses, though," Clay pointed out.

"That's unfortunate, of course, but surely the cattle are more important?"

"No," Clay said.

I appreciated that, because the cattle were more important to him.

"There's this mare that's kind of important to me," I said. "There's also the fact that Lee would know where the other six hundred head were going."

"Now that he knows there's someone after

him, we've sort of lost the element of surprise," Clay added.

The sheriff nodded. "Well, I can understand that that might worry you. But as for the mare, I got a pretty good look at those horses. I didn't see anything all that special except the bronco."

"Bronco?" I said. "There wasn't anything like that in our remuda."

"Sure," the sheriff said. "Little chestnut mare, looked as mild as you please, but just let anybody try to get on her back and watch out!"

"That's the one," I said. "Who was trying to ride her?"

"Why, just about everybody," Charlie said. "I gave it a try myself. But why's she so special? What good is a horse you can't ride?"

"You can't ride her. *I* can. What do you mean, nearly everybody?"

I guess I was looking a little upset, because Clay put his hand on my arm like he thought he might have to hold me back.

"Lee was taking bets," the mayor said. "Offered twenty dollars to anyone who could stay on her for a full minute. Then he took bets from anyone who had two bits to wager. She looked so small and mild that he got quite a few takers at first. After a while no one else was interested until finally Ben tried it."

"Why, that son of a— And who is this Ben?"

"Ben's our trick rider. Naturally he didn't have any trouble staying on at all."

I took a deep breath to calm down, then said, "Could you hold it a minute there, Mr. Hawk? You sort of lost me. Why do you have a trick rider, and why is it *natural* that he stayed on?"

The mayor looked a little embarrassed. "This town isn't exactly your usual cow town, Mr. Johnson. Suppose we go back into town and have breakfast. I'll tell you about it, and maybe we can decide what to do about your herd."

I had a few more questions ready, but Clay nodded. "All right," he said. He turned his horse and started back the way we'd come, and I followed.

As we rode back into town I noticed something I'd missed on the way out. Near the edge of town was a big white tent. It had a bunch of colored streamers hanging from the guy wires and the entrance, and from inside it I could hear voices shouting and horses snorting.

"Circus in town?" I asked.

The sheriff grinned and again the mayor looked almost embarrassed.

"That's what I was going to tell you," he admitted.

"It's interesting, but—" Clay started to say.

"We might as well stop and have breakfast

here," the mayor said firmly, pulling up his horse and dismounting.

I was starting to get a little confused. I caught Clay's eye and he shrugged, so I swung down from Binny and followed the others into the tent.

Sure enough, it was a circus. There weren't any stands set up around the edges, but there was a big red-painted ring in the center and trapezes and a tightrope up above. Six white horses with plumes were tethered at one side of the ring, and a dozen or more people were just sitting down to breakfast at a big table set up in the middle of the ring. There wasn't one of them that didn't have glitter and sequins scattered all over his or her clothes. Most of the women had plumes just like the horses' and none of them was wearing quite as much as I was used to seeing on a lady. I wasn't quite sure where to look, so I settled on the mayor.

"Look, this is real interesting, but could you please come to the point, whatever it is? I'm starting to get confused."

"Of course," the mayor said. "If you'll both just take a seat at the table."

"I don't want to—"

"Come on, Luke," Clay interrupted. "I'm hungry, and he isn't going to tell us a thing until he's got us sitting down."

"All right," I said. "Anything to find out what's going on."

We went over and took some of the empty seats at the table. The circus people looked at Clay and me a little curiously, but they didn't seem the least bit surprised when three of the citizens of the town they were playing in dropped by for breakfast.

The mayor gave them all a big good morning, then turned back to us.

"Help yourselves," he said, gesturing to the big platters of ham and eggs and biscuits that lined the table. "Well, Mr. Johnson, you asked me if the circus had come to town. The fact is that the circus *is* the town. The name of our town, gentlemen, is Big Top. Everyone in this town was, until a few years ago, a performer in or employee of Jason Hawk's Circus of the Americas."

I couldn't think of a thing to say to that, and I think even Clay was at a loss for words. Finally, seeing that we weren't going to say anything, Hawk went on:

"Three years ago I decided to bring the circus farther west than we usually went. Things were booming out here, and it stood to reason, we thought, that the circus would do well. And we did, too, for the first part of the tour. Then things took a turn. We got to one of the scheduled towns and there was no one there. It was completely deserted. We realized later that everyone had packed up and headed into the mountains to look for gold, but meanwhile we had no idea what had happened. We decided to go on to the next town, but we never made it. A storm came up and we were lost for days. Even after the rain stopped, the clouds were so heavy we couldn't tell which direction was west. Our guide had been lost crossing a river and he had our only compass.

"We kept moving because we didn't know what else to do. Finally we ended up back at the ghost town. And we decided to stay. At first we just wanted a chance to assess our situation. The people who'd abandoned the place had left enough things in the way of tools and such, so that with what we already had we were able to stay alive that first winter and keep ourselves and the animals fed.

"By the next spring we realized that we were sitting pretty. I'd been right to think that a circus could do pretty well out here, but it made a lot more sense to have our headquarters right here in the middle of this territory. In the winter we're storekeepers and sheriffs and farmers and ranchers, but every spring we send out the Big Top."

Well, that was just about the strangest thing I'd ever heard, and I guess I must have looked it because the mayor started laughing.

"That's what we wanted the beef for, of course," he said when he'd recovered a little. "The wagons are just about to head out, and we wanted to stock up for the big cats and also leave some here in town. We haven't had a chance to build up much of a herd yet."

"I guess that explains why you have a trick rider," I said. "It still doesn't really explain how he was able to stay on Liz for a minute."

"That kid can ride anything," the sheriff said.

"Kid?"

"Yeah. He can't be more than fourteen, if he's that."

"Don't you know?" Clay asked.

The sheriff shook his head. "He came riding in here two years ago on an old piebald mare. You never saw such a sad-looking horse. The kid looked hungry so we took him in and that night we let him watch one of our dress rehearsals. The next thing we knew he went scooting out after that old mare and brought her into the tent. Before we had time to turn around, he had her doing tricks and dance steps all over the place."

"A circus can always use someone who can handle animals like that," the mayor said, taking up the story. "So when he seemed to want to stay on, we were only too glad to have him.

Since then he's handled all our horses, and he's never had any trouble with any of them. That's why he was able to ride your horse. That mare had gotten rid of six or seven others without a whole lot of trouble, but when he got into the saddle she didn't even try to ditch him. He just whispered in her ear and off they went."

I looked at them doubtfully. That just wasn't like Liz. She'd only once in her life let anyone but me ride her and that was Clay. And at that, I'd been leading her. It might be because the circus rider was a kid that she'd let him stay on. I'd noticed before that both dogs and horses were apt to allow kids a lot more leeway than they did adults.

"I'd like to talk to this—what did you say his name is?"

"We call him Ben," Charlie said. "Only, there's a problem with talking to him."

"What's that?"

"He doesn't talk," Charlie said. "We don't know if he can't or just won't. We once had a doctor look him over, and there wasn't anything wrong that he could find, but Ben still doesn't say anything. I thought I heard him talking in his sleep once," he added thoughtfully.

I shook my head. "I'm getting confused again," I told them. "Could I see him, anyway?

I take it he'll understand what I'm saying to him?"

"Sure," the sheriff said. He turned to a man dressed in a clown suit sitting next to him. "Have you seen Ben, Lucas?"

The clown just shook his head, and I wondered if he couldn't talk, either.

"Anybody here seen Ben?" the sheriff asked, raising his voice.

"Not since last night," said a plump, motherly sort of woman with a bullwhip coiled around her neck.

"That's funny," the mayor said. "He was definitely on call for this morning. I wanted to watch him go through the Roman-candle routine."

"Do you work with the circus too?" I asked curiously.

"Of course," he said. "I'm the ringmaster."

"I should have guessed," I muttered.

"Charlie, would you go and see if Ben is at Mrs. Miner's place?" the sheriff asked. "That's where he lives," he explained to Clay and me.

"Sure," Charlie said. "I've got a half hour or so before I need to get to work."

"What do you do?" I asked, almost afraid to find out.

"This and that," he told me with a grin.

"Right now I'm a tightrope walker and the sword swallower."

"Now then," the mayor said as Charlie left, "maybe we could talk a little business. We'd still like to buy those cattle."

Clay frowned. "What were you going to give the rustler for them?" he asked. "The price is high this year at the railhead."

"He'd asked twenty."

Clay shook his head. "That's a little low. We don't expect to get what we would at the railhead, of course, but we have to have at least twenty-four."

I didn't move a muscle. We were the next thing to broke, and we had to keep following Lee if we were ever going to get either the horses or the rest of the cattle back. Some people might have figured that that was a good-enough reason to take twenty dollars a head, but Clay evidently didn't plan on taking any bigger loss than we had to on this.

"That's a little high," the mayor said.

Clay didn't answer that. He just sat there.

After a minute the mayor sighed. "All right. I can tell when a man's stubborner than I am. Twenty-four. That's forty-eight hundred for the lot of them."

"That'll be fine," Clay said. "Now, what are

the chances that you can give us a little help tracking these fellas down, sheriff?"

The sheriff shook his head. "I'd like to, but the wagons start out tomorrow."

"What does that mean?" I asked.

"Don is our strongman and also our wagon master," the mayor said. "Sheriffing is strictly part time for him."

I could see that Clay was getting ready to protest this interpretation of a sheriff's responsibilities when Charlie ran back into the tent.

"He's gone!" he announced. "Mrs. Miner says that he ran off. He wasn't there this morning when she got up."

"Why didn't she let me know?" the sheriff snapped.

"I guess she didn't realize that he wasn't over here working until I asked about him. Besides, you know that she doesn't get up all that early anymore. She'd just finished trimming her beard when I got there."

"Huh?" I said.

"She's the bearded lady," Charlie explained. "She shaves when we aren't on the road, and she's been getting her beard back into shape the last month or so. It takes a little work. Anyway, I checked his room, and all his stuff's there except just what he was wearing."

"He must have gone off with Lee," the sheriff said. "What on earth do you suppose possessed him to do that?"

"What makes you think he went of his own accord?" Charlie asked.

"Can you think of any reason a bunch of outlaws would want to take along a fourteen-year-old boy who doesn't talk?" the mayor asked.

"No, but that doesn't mean they don't have one," Charlie said. "We'll have to go after him."

"Be reasonable, Charlie, will you?" the sheriff snapped. "The wagons leave tomorrow. We have to be on them. We just finished telling these two that."

Charlie frowned at him, then transferred the frown to Clay and me. "Are you going after them?"

"That's right," Clay said.

"Then I'm going with you," Charlie said. "I'm not letting any fourteen-year-old boy go off with a bunch of rustlers whether it was his idea or theirs."

"What about your acts, you idiot?" the sheriff said.

"Jennie can handle the high wire, and Pete can swallow the swords when he isn't being the mysterious mystic from Manchuria." Charlie turned back to us. "I can be ready in two hours," he said.

Clay and I exchanged glances. We'd hoped for more help than this, but we couldn't hope for anyone more determined.

"Glad to have you, Charlie," I said. "All I can say is, I hope you can cook better than we can."

Chapter Ten

The rain kept up for two more days, but at least this time we had slickers to keep it off. We weren't exactly a lighthearted crew, what with worrying about cows and horses and the kid, but we weren't doing too bad. We spoke to each other three or four times a day, and once I was pretty sure I heard Clay whistling.

On the third day the weather let up and the sun came out.

"Well," Clay said, looking up at the blue sky, "now maybe we can find out if we've been going the right way. Keep an eye out for tracks, you two."

"It could be a while before we spot any," Charlie pointed out.

"Looking won't make it any longer," Clay said a little sharply. Like I said, none of us was at our best.

We started to pick up some tracks along toward evening. They'd been made before the

101

rain stopped, but they hadn't been washed away entirely.

"Now, if they're just the right ones," I muttered.

After another mile I knew that they were. There was a hoofprint from Clay's big gelding just as clear as could be.

"It's them," I said. "These were made after it stopped raining."

"We couldn't be more than a day or two behind," Clay said, getting down and examining the tracks more closely.

"Now what?" I asked.

"What do you mean?" Charlie asked. "We've got 'em."

"There's still only three of us—and at least six of them."

"How do you know that?"

"There were three of them in Big Top, right?"

"Right."

"And we killed one," I said. "That leaves two. If there were three of them with two hundred head, then there were at least four with the other part of the herd. That's six. Do we holler for the law?" I asked Clay.

He shrugged. "If we can find any and if they want to help, that's fine. On the other hand, our luck hasn't been too good that way so far."

"So maybe we ought to have some kind of plan in case we don't get help," I said.

"Yeah," Clay agreed. "It's just that I can't think of one."

"Of course we could always wait until they'd sold the cattle and then go in and claim them."

"That probably wouldn't set too well with the people who bought them," Clay pointed out.

"I guess it wouldn't," I agreed. "We're likely to get killed that way."

"That's fine for the cattle," Charlie said, "but what about Ben and the horses? That won't get them back."

"I was going to get to that," I told him. "Do you have any ideas?"

"Why not do what you did in Big Top? Get there and state your claim before they sell the cattle. The buyer will have to check into it then, whether he wants to or not. At the same time, I can get Ben and you can get your horses."

"I guess the first thing to do is find them," Clay said firmly. "For all we know they've already sold the cattle and are halfway to Mexico."

That seemed a little unlikely, but I got the point. There wasn't much use planning until we knew what we were planning for.

"All right, Clay, be reasonable if you want to."

He looked over at me and grinned. "Never mind," he told me consolingly. "I don't intend to be one bit more reasonable than you'll be when we catch up with 'em. Let's go."

After another couple of miles we started seeing cattle. Not ours, but some nice, fat critters, most of them with nice, fat calves at their sides. The brand on most of them seemed to be the Double Diamond, though there was a fair sprinkling of others.

"Looks like we're coming to a pretty fair-sized spread," I commented after we'd gone a few miles, with the cattle gettting more and more numerous.

"Looks like they wintered pretty well too," Clay observed.

"Is that smoke up there?" Charlie asked abruptly.

"Looks like it," Clay said, peering ahead intently. "We'd better check. It's probably just a branding fire, but. . . ."

The "but" didn't need any expanding on. A range fire was the last thing that anyone even remotely connected with ranching wants to see. If this was one, it was still small enough so that we might be able to deal with it. If it was a branding fire, no harm done and we might get news of our herd.

It wasn't too far to that fire, and long before we got there it was clear that whatever it was, this fire was man-made and under control. We let the horses slacken their speed a little and came up to the fire at a cautious trot.

Clay pulled up about a hundred feet out, just so they wouldn't feel crowded. It was a branding fire, all right, and the men around it looked pretty busy, but one fella had noticed us, and he came toward us with his rifle cradled in the crook of his arm.

"Something I can do to help you fellas?" he asked, not looking like he cared to all that much.

"Could be," Clay said. "We saw the smoke from your fire. We thought it might be a good idea to come and make sure it wasn't a range fire getting started."

"It's under control," he said, but I thought he seemed a bit less hostile.

"So I see," Clay said. "You wouldn't have seen a herd of about six hundred with a C Bar L going through here in the last day or two, would you?" he added. "That's what we're out here looking for."

I didn't think the man looked all that happy to hear it, but he didn't hesitate.

"I haven't seen any herd but the one that belongs here," he said. "Trail herds aren't encouraged to cross Double Diamond range."

Clay nodded thoughtfully. I had a feeling he wasn't the least bit surprised to hear it. "Is there a town near here?" he asked.

"Two. Which one did you have in mind? The one with the railroad spur line or the one with the two churches?"

"I guess the one with the spur line would be of more immediate use," Clay said. "How did it happen to get the spur, anyway?"

"It's in the foothills just below the Lucky Lucifer mine. It makes it pretty handy for shipping cattle too, though."

"I can imagine it would," Clay said. "Good, fat ones too. It must make quite a difference in what you get for 'em."

The other man nodded. "We don't have to walk half the fat off 'em. Anyway, the name of the town is Armbuster, and it's about half a day's ride to the west. Just head that way and you'll cut across a road that'll take you straight into town."

"Is that the way a herd that was going around Double Diamond land would take?" Charlie asked.

"If they'd known about it, they'd have swung wide back there," he said, pointing the way we'd come. "Otherwise, they would have gotten an escort."

"You think they might have?" I asked.

"Could be," he said. "If you tracked them

this far, then they probably got spotted a little ahead. One thing is sure. They didn't go all the way through to town on this range." He shifted his rifle a little. "Mind if I ask a few questions?"

"I guess not," Clay said. "We sure asked enough."

"Then you might just tell me who you are and what you want with that herd."

That seemed fair enough to me, but Clay didn't see it that way. "My name's Jack Moore," he said without any hesitation at all. "These two are my cousins Paul and Tom. A couple of weeks ago Tom's son ran off. We've got a notion he's with that herd, and we'd sort of like to catch up with him."

"Is he a pretty young kid?" the man asked, probably thinking that if the kid had enough gumption to take off on a cattle drive, then we ought to just let him try it.

"Fourteen," Clay said, "but it's not his age so much. The thing is that he can't talk, and his mother gets pretty worried. Paul and I were coming this way anyhow, so we told Tom we'd help him look."

The man nodded. "Well, I wish you luck. My name's John Collins. Like I said, I haven't seen anything of that herd, but it stands to reason that if they were trailing this way, they must have had it in mind either to sell to the mines or ship out on the spur line. Probably ship," he added. "We keep the mines pretty well supplied."

"Thanks for the information," I said. "We appreciate it."

We turned our horses to the west and set off again. This time, though, I was starting to feel more optimistic. We'd been wondering why Lee was heading this way ever since he took the cattle, and now we knew. A feeder line to the mine made it a perfect place for him to ship his cattle. The only thing that was puzzling me was why we hadn't known there was a shipping point this close to home.

"This could save us a couple of weeks' driving next year, Clay."

"Yeah. I'm surprised we haven't heard about it. It must be pretty new."

"Never mind that," Charlie said. "Do you think we'll find Ben here?"

"Seems likely," Clay said. "We couldn't have been too far behind, and they had to go around the Double Diamond. Besides that, it takes a little while to sell a herd of cattle."

We rode hard, trying to make it before nightfall to the road we'd been told about. We made it to the edges of Armbuster just as the last rays of the sun failed.

"Pretty good-sized town," Clay commented.

"Well, it's got its own spur line," I pointed

out. "Look there, Clay. That house has a picket fence."

"The one next to it has a knocker on the door," he said, obviously not wanting to be outdone in his powers of observing architecture.

"We play here every year with the circus," Charlie said casually. "They've got a pretty nice hotel."

"How come you didn't mention the railroad to us?" Clay asked.

Charlie shrugged. "I don't think they had it last year. For that matter, I'm not quite certain why it's so important."

"I thought Hawk said you people raise cattle in Big Top too."

"Not me," Charlie said firmly.

"Well, whenever you've got cattle, you've got to get them to market. The faster you can do that, the higher the price is likely to be. But if you drive them too fast, then they lose weight and you can't get such a good price. On the other hand, if you just put them in a railroad car, they don't lose much weight and they get to market faster. That way you make more money. So if you can steal cattle and drive them to a nearby spur line, then you're really making money."

"I guess I've got quite a lot to learn about cattle and cattle rustlers," Charlie said with a wry grin. "Now, how do you feel about that hotel?"

"Maybe we ought to take a look in the holding pens first," I said. "I'd hate to find out that those cattle were all shipped out while we were munching on a piece of apple pie."

"You're the boss," Charlie said cheerfully. "I'll tell you what. You go put the horses in the livery stable near the hotel, and I'll reserve us a couple of rooms. Then we can go right over to where they hold the cattle."

"Suits me," Clay said.

Charlie dismounted and handed me the reins of his horse, saying, "I'll meet you by the railroad station when I'm finished." Then he turned and started down the street.

"Kind of abrupt sometimes, isn't he?" Clay commented. "I'd sort of had a notion we might ride, but if he's counting on us putting the horses in the livery stable, we might just as well do it."

"It might not be such a bad idea to look over the horses they have stabled, anyway," I said. "Maybe we'll meet someone we know."

With a sort of interested look in his eye, Clay headed his gelding down the street toward the stable.

I'll say one thing for Armbuster. It was the busiest town we'd seen yet. There were people all over the streets even though it was just about suppertime, and all the stores looked pretty prosperous. When we got to the stable there were three boys working there in addition to the owner, and he didn't have any stall space left.

"I can turn 'em into the corral for you and make sure they get a nose bag of grain and some hay, but that's about it," he told us. "I haven't got a square inch of space left inside."

"Rub 'em down good and you've got a deal," I said. "Is it always this busy around here?"

"Not quite, but this town is booming, make no mistake."

"Mind if we look around a little?" Clay asked. "I've been thinking of getting a new horse, and this looks like a good place to start."

The man looked interested. "Sure," he said. "I've got a gelding over here that—"

Before he had a chance to really get started, one of the boys stuck his head out from behind the barn and hollered for some help. The owner looked irritated but he went.

"You never know what these boys are going to get up to," he apologized. "Just look around. I'll be back as quick as I can."

"Take your time," Clay told him. "We aren't in any hurry."

"Oh, yes, we are," I said to Clay as the livery man hurried off. "We've got to hurry up and check the stable before he comes back."

"Shouldn't take long. If any of our horses are in here, we'll know 'em right off."

We slipped into the stable. Sure enough, the place had horses in every stall and a few tied up where there weren't any stalls. The place was just as full as the owner had told us. The only problem was that not one of the horses belonged to us.

"Oh, well," Clay said as we went back out through the door. "It would have been too easy, I guess."

"I wouldn't have minded that just for once."

He shook his head sadly. "You're getting soft, Luke."

"See anything you like, mister?" The owner of the stables had apparently finished with his helper.

"A few," Clay said cautiously. "I'd better come back in daylight, though. It's a little hard to get a good look by lantern light."

"That's true. Well, whenever you're ready I'll be here. Chuck Jansen's the name." He stuck out a hand the size of a small ham.

"Pleased to meet you." Clay shook hands with him. "We'll probably be back in the morning."

We headed off down the street before Jansen

had a chance to notice that Clay hadn't given him *his* name.

"What was that all about?" I asked.

"I couldn't remember the name I'd told that guy out on the range," Clay said.

"I guess it wouldn't do to go around handing out a different name to everyone we meet," I agreed. "I suppose we couldn't use our right names?"

Clay shook his head. "Those men I hired wouldn't be too likely to forget my name, and they might remember yours too."

I frowned. "You were Jack Moore and I was Paul, but I'll be darned if I remember what you called Charlie."

"He was Tom," Clay reminded me. "Do you think we should write the names down?"

"That might be a good idea. You got a pencil?"

He pulled a stub out of his pocket, along with a scrap of paper, and jotted down the names. "Okay," he said. "Let's head for the railroad station."

As it turned out, the station was at the other end of the town. If I'd known that, I wouldn't have been quite so quick to leave the horses at the stable. We'd ridden all day, we were tired, and riding boots aren't very good for walking.

"If I get a blister out of this, I'm not going to be any too happy," I muttered.

"You won't unless you have a hole in your sock," Clay told me. "Not if your boots fit."

I looked at him in exasperation. "Have you ever known me not to have a hole in my sock?"

"Luke, it's a perfectly simple thing to learn to darn a sock. It's also perfectly simple to buy new socks. Why don't you do one or the other?"

"I haven't had the time to buy a lot of socks lately," I pointed out. I didn't figure the other part of what he'd said was even worth commenting on.

"Then get in there and buy some," he said, grabbing my arm and hauling me toward a dry-goods store.

"Charlie will be waiting for us," I protested.

"Let him wait. He doesn't complain as much as you do."

For a minute I considered losing my temper, then realized that I didn't really have any call to.

"All right," I said. "You're right. We'll go buy socks."

He shook his head. "Never mind. Complain all you want to. I'm just getting a little tired."

"That makes two of us. Let's forget the socks and have a beer."

"I don't know that we want to make Charlie wait that long," Clay said with a sudden grin.

By the time we got to the station it was completely dark. The holding pens were supposed to be a couple of hundred yards beyond the station building and I could hear the cattle lowing, but I couldn't see a thing.

"How are we supposed to tell whose cattle those are in the dark?" I asked Clay.

"I've got some matches. All we have to do is get close enough to read one brand."

That sounded reasonable enough. "Light one now so that we can see where we're going," I said. "The ground isn't any too even here."

"Hang on a minute," he told me.

About to comment that we should have brought a lantern, I suddenly realized that we weren't alone.

"Watch it, Clay," I whispered. "There's someone else here."

There was a muffled curse in the darkness and something whistled through the air next to my head—a club, from the sound of it. I ducked away from it and smashed into what was probably the side of the station.

Before I had a chance to straighten up, the club whistled through the air again and this time connected with my shoulder. My shoulder went numb and I hit the ground, partly to get out of the way and partly because I didn't have any choice.

I could hear the sound of scuffling in the dark, and I realized that Clay was having problems of his own. That meant that I'd better figure out how to handle the fellow with the club. A boot connected with my wrist. I rolled away from the boot and the building, then tried to get to my feet. It wasn't that easy, but I made it before whoever was bashing me managed to figure out where I'd gone. I staggered off a few feet and yanked out my gun. My left arm didn't seem to have any feeling in it at all. Now, if I could just see where to shoot, I'd be all set.

I didn't have much chance to worry about it. I had the gun out in front of me as I peered into the darkness, and suddenly someone walked right into it. I don't know who was more surprised, me or him.

I got the use of my voice back first. "You hold it right there, mister," I said, trying to sound as mean as I could, which by that time wasn't too hard. "If you so much as twitch, I'll put a hole right through you."

Naturally, the sensible thing for him to do would have been to hold still. But the thing is, when you walk into a gun in the dark and someone threatens to make holes in you, you're likely to be a little surprised, and surprised people don't often do the sensible thing. Instead of holding still, he took a wild swing at me that somehow managed to connect with the side of my jaw and knocked me silly. Just before hitting the ground, I heard the boom of a .38, which, I had a notion, was mine.

Chapter Eleven

The next thing I really noticed was that someone was punching me in the belly. Not hard, just steadily. I raised my hand to object and found that I couldn't move it. That seemed pretty peculiar, and after giving it a little thought I decided that I was tied to something. Another few minutes, and I decided that what I was tied to was a horse and that no one was punching me. I was tied face down across a horse and he was trotting. I felt sort of pleased with myself for working it out until I realized that no one in my position had any right to feel pleased with anything.

Once I'd gotten that far I opened my eyes to see what was going on. That was a mistake. There's nothing like seeing the ground rushing by a few feet under your nose to make you appreciate a little ignorance. I let out a yell and shut my eyes again as quickly as I could.

"He's awake," a voice growled to my left.

"So I heard," another voice said. "What do you want me to do about it?"

"Shouldn't we blindfold him or something?"

"I don't really see much point in it, but you go ahead if it makes you feel any better."

Somehow I had the feeling that what they were saying was pretty important, and once I felt a little better I thought I might be able to figure out why. I was pretty sure I wasn't in the best shape I'd ever been in. My head pounded and my stomach was feeling pretty awful and I could hardly feel my hands and feet at all. Not only that but it was raining again and I was cold, miserable, and afraid.

"I don't see why we don't just kill him," a new voice said.

For a second I felt like my heart had stopped beating, and I hoped that somebody would give him a reason pretty quick for keeping me alive.

"Because he isn't the only one. We aren't ready to move out of here yet. We got to have something to keep his partner from going to the law."

"Why don't we get his partner too?"

The second voice said in exasperation, "We tried that, remember?"

I didn't like the sound of all that, but at least it seemed like they weren't planning anything too drastic right away. All I had to do was shake loose from them before they got ready to leave.

"What makes you think his partner hasn't already gone to the law?"

"That's being taken care of," the other voice said. "How many times do we have to go over this?"

Apparently that was the last time, because everyone stopped talking and left me to suffer in silence. I tried opening my eyes again, but it was nearly as bad as the first time. After that, I kept them closed and wished we'd get where we were going. It stood to reason that nothing could be as bad as hanging upside down over the back of a horse.

I tried to pull myself together a little. From what they'd said, they'd tried to kill both Clay and me. Somehow, they must have spotted us when we got to the station. Clay would have been easy for them to recognize. When they'd seen that he was going to get away, they'd taken me with them to use as a hostage instead of killing me. They evidently hadn't managed to sell the cattle yet, and they wanted a way to keep Clay under control until they did. Later they'd finish me off without a second thought.

All of which made it seem like a good idea to get away as soon as I could. *If* I could. So far I didn't have any ideas. I didn't even know where I was. It was clear that we were riding over rough ground and we seemed to be going uphill most of the time, but since we were in mining country that didn't really tell me a lot.

"Go easy," a voice said up ahead. My horse hung back against his reins for a second and then abruptly plunged forward. The air suddenly filled with dust and gravel, stinging against my skin, and I realized that we were heading down a steep, shale-covered slope. My horse was half sliding on his haunches, and my hands and feet were taking quite a beating against the sharp particles of rock. Not only that but my head was an awful lot closer to the ground than I was really comfortable with. If that horse slipped just a little, my brains were going to be scattered all over this hillside. I'd started thinking that this would be a darn good time to be somewhere else when all of a sudden there was a pop and the rope tying my ankles to my wrist gave way.

I grabbed wildly at the horse although I could scarcely move my fingers. By some miracle I got one hand twisted in the horse's mane and managed to swing one of my legs over its back. Thrown off balance, the horse snorted wildly and scrabbled at the shale, trying to keep his feet under him. Somehow he succeeded.

My head was reeling and I felt like I had scratches all over my body from the shale. At the same time, things had changed a little. My hands were free and I was on a horse. It seemed to me like I ought to take advantage of that situation. The reins were still in the hands of the man in front of me and I made a grab for them around the horse's neck. I got a good hold on them and yanked. The results were even better than I could have hoped for. Apparently that hombre had wrapped the reins around his hand, because when I yanked, I pulled him off balance. A second later he was flailing wildly as he left his saddle.

My mount swerved to the right to avoid him, and I managed to stay in the saddle as I pulled the reins up over his head.

I got control just about as we reached the bottom of the slope, and I didn't waste any time. I didn't know where I was, but I had a pretty good idea that we'd gone up into the mountains, so I pointed that pony's nose downhill around the edge of the slope and gave him a kick. He took off, and I flattened myself out along his back as much as I could so that I wouldn't make too good a target.

There was a shout behind me and a bullet suddenly whistled past my head.

"Don't kill him!" someone shouted.

That sounded like a good idea to me. They couldn't want me alive any more than I did, and I figured that it gave me a better chance to get away.

I took advantage of it. I kept my horse moving as fast as it was safe for him to go on that kind of footing, or maybe a little faster, and kept heading downhill. The others were behind me. I could hear their horses, but they didn't sound like they were getting any closer. Of course, they had the advantage of knowing where they were.

The circulation was starting to come back into my hands and feet now. That probably should have made it easier to stay on the horse, but it was pretty painful and somehow it didn't help a bit.

On the other hand, I was pulling ahead of them a little. Maybe I'd finally gotten lucky. I had the fastest horse and if I was able to find the town before it gave out, I might just make it.

Still heading downhill, I was starting to see signs of a trail ahead of me. I liked the look of that, and I liked it even better when I rounded a clump of spruce and found that my trail joined up with a heavily traveled one. With any luck at all, this one would head back toward town.

My horse was starting to slow a little, and I decided he was getting pretty tired. We'd been on the move all night and at least an hour into daylight. I pulled up a little, hoping the horses behind me were in the same shape. If they weren't, I was done for.

My horse seemed grateful for the letup. He loped along at an easy pace while I listened nervously for hoofbeats behind me and wished my headache would go away. After about five minutes I heard them coming, still faint but getting louder.

That seemed like enough dawdling to me. I gave the pony a kick, and he responded instantly, as though the breather had been all he needed. And then his gait faltered. He took up the pace again, but there was no question in my mind that he'd picked up a stone or something. He was definitely favoring his left foreleg.

And that takes care of that, I thought glumly. If I kept riding him, he'd pull up lame and it wouldn't take more than a few minutes for those rustlers to catch up with me.

I considered my alternatives and decided I really had only one. I pulled the horse up and dismounted. My knees buckled a little as I put my weight on them, but I held myself up against the saddle for a minute and pretty soon I felt like I might be able to take a step or two if I was real careful about it.

"Come on, horse," I muttered, leading him toward a thick grove of pine trees. If I could get myself out of sight before they caught up, they might go right on past me.

There were enough old hoofprints on the dust of the trail so they might not notice where a set headed off toward the trees. I considered wiping them out after I had the horse hidden, then decided against it. They might get here too quickly for that.

The pine grove was thick and grew back onto the hillside. It ought to be pretty good cover, I decided, as I led the pony up through the trees. I moved up until I couldn't see the trail anymore, then figured that that ought to mean that no one on the trail could see me, either. I took a quick look at the horse's hoof while I was at it. Sure enough, there was a small stone wedged against the frog. I pried at the stone without much hope of budging it, but it popped right out in my hand. For a second I considered heading down the trail again, but the hoofbeats were getting too close. I took a firm grip on the horse and got ready to make sure he didn't decide to whinny a greeting when his stablemates came closer.

The hoofbeats were getting louder now, although for some reason they sounded like they were coming from down trail instead of up, and moving a lot slower than I would have expected.

I peered off in that direction, wondering if it

could be someone else I was hearing. It was. I could just glimpse the trail in that direction, and suddenly a rider swept into view. It was Clay.

That made things a little bit different. I grabbed at the reins and swung myself into the saddle. If Clay passed me, he was likely to ride right into the arms of the guys who were following me.

I headed down through the trees and came sliding out onto the trail just in front of Clay and Charlie.

"Luke! I thought—"

"I got away! Never mind that. They're just behind me, and I think it might be a good idea if we got out of here."

"Back down the trail or up into the trees?" Clay asked.

I hesitated, then shook my head. "You decide. I don't know where we are or what's around the next bend."

"Down the trail, then," Clay said decisively. "If they get too close, we'll have to fight it out."

"Wouldn't it be better to try to negotiate with them?" Charlie asked. "After all, they have Ben."

"Their general plan is to kill us," I told him. "Clay and me, that is. You weren't at the station, so they probably don't realize that you're with us. I don't think they'd listen to any deals we might have in mind."

Clay turned his horse. "Let's go,' he said. "We don't have time to talk about it here."

He was right about that, anyway. This time the hoofbeats were coming from up trail and they were getting louder all the time.

"All right," Charlie agreed. "We can figure out what to do next once we get away."

He turned his horse to follow Clay, with me right behind him.

Chapter Twelve

"Do you think they might have a marshal here?" I asked as we rode down the main street of Armbuster. "Someone with a little more territory than that last fella?"

"Not the way our luck has been going," Clay said. "I wonder if we should even bother."

"You're not planning to just forget about it, are you?" Charlie asked.

"Of course he isn't," I said. "He's just planning to do it all himself."

Charlie nodded. "That might not be such a bad idea. All we'd have to do is—"

"Am I the only one here who isn't crazy?" I asked. "We just figured out that there are at least six of them, not counting that kid of yours. They know we're here. They have plans to kill us. To me, that sounds like we need help. What does it sound like to you?"

"Well," Clay said mildly, "so far we've gotten back part of the herd, we know where they

129

are, and we're still alive. To me that sounds like at least a tie. On the other hand, we've talked to two sheriffs and got nothing but a little information. And that sounds like a waste of time."

"You got something in mind?" I asked.

"Yeah," he said. "We didn't get a chance to look at those brands, but I don't think there's any doubt that they're C Bar L, do you?"

"I guess not."

"They might take off without those cattle and without getting paid for them, but I kinda tend to doubt it. Those cattle pens are right at the focus of this. We can go to the sheriff or marshal and say those are our cattle, and maybe he'll believe us and maybe he won't. He'll probably hold the cattle until he finds out, but what happens in the meantime?"

I thought about it. "The rustlers find out what's going on and they fade out."

"Yeah, with the kid and the remuda, which means Liz."

"All right. What's the other way to do it?"

"We wait until they try to take either the herd or the money and we follow them. As soon as we find Liz and the kid, then we get the law."

"And suppose the law decides we're lying?"

"Well," Clay said, "that's where the other part of the plan comes in. We don't wait until then to get proof that C Bar L is our brand. I didn't notice any telegraph lines when we first rode in, but this spur line probably has one. If it doesn't, it probably isn't all that far down the line to a place that does. One of us goes off and wires the Cattlemen's Association to send confirmation of the brand registration. We'll have it sent right to the sheriff's office."

"That's a great idea," Charlie said enthusiastically. "Who'll go?"

"You will," I said.

"But—"

"No buts," I told him. "Clay was the sheriff in our town for the last two years. Unless you can prove to me that you can handle a rifle better than I can, you're elected."

"But you wouldn't recognize Ben," he protested sort of weakly.

"Charlie, just how many fourteen-year-old kids who can't talk do you think we're going to run in to?"

"I guess you're right," he said. "I'll leave as soon as I get cleaned up a little."

"Don't be too quick," Clay said. "We still don't know that there isn't a telegraph office in town."

Charlie nodded. "That's right. I'll go look for it now and meet you over at the hotel."

I remembered that he'd gone to book us

rooms earlier. I just hoped they hadn't given up on us.

"Which way is the hotel?" I asked.

"Just keep down this street. It's called the End of the Line."

"Great," I muttered. "Let's hope it isn't."

Charlie turned his horse away and headed back the way we'd come.

"It occurs to me that we ought to have someone out at the cattle pens," I said to Clay as we started along the street again. "They may decide not to wait now that they've lost us."

Clay nodded. "We'll have to do this in shifts. I'd better take the first one. You look a little the worse for wear."

I shook my head. "I got part of a night's sleep, at least," I pointed out. "You were up trailing me."

"I don't know that I'd call being knocked unconscious a night's sleep, and you look sort of like someone's been sticking pins in you," Clay said. "But if you think you're okay to start watching, then we might as well both go out there now."

"Let's grab something to take with us at that bakery," I suggested.

"Okay, I guess I could eat a little something," he agreed.

As soon as we stepped inside, I realized just how hungry I was. Every good smell in the world seemed to be looking for room in my nose, and a plump, pretty little woman was standing behind a glass counter that was piled high with every imaginable sort of doughnut and pie and cake.

"Good morning," she said with a smile. "Is there something I can get for you two?"

"Doughnuts," Clay said before I could get a word in. "How about a couple of dozen of those in the front?"

"Of course." She smiled. "They're fresh out of the kettle. Still warm, I wouldn't wonder."

"That sounds fine to me. Okay with you, Luke?"

By that time I wasn't listening, though. My attention was on a broadside that had been put up on the plank wall next to the counter.

"Never mind doughnuts," I snapped. "Take a look at this."

He moved over beside me and we both stared at it.

RIDE THE BRONC! we read. *Pay $1 to ride the bronc and win $100!*

There was a lot more, but I didn't need to read it. That horse had to be Liz, and she was going to have every fool drunk in town trying to ride her. A sort of red haze settled in front of my eyes as I started out of the shop, but I was stopped by a hand on my arm.

"Just hold on a minute, Luke. This ain't no time to go off half-cocked."

"The heck it ain't," I said between gritted teeth, yanking my arm away.

"Luke, you listen to me. You go busting around like this, and all you're going to get is killed. If you use your head, we can get Liz back."

That slowed me down for a second, and as soon as I thought about it I could see that he was right. I turned back toward the counter, where the woman was looking concerned and maybe a little frightened.

"Sorry, ma'am," I said. "I guess we'd like those doughnuts after all if it isn't too much trouble."

I guess it wasn't, because she put them in a waxed-paper sack and took our money. We headed out the door and started back toward the cattle pen.

"This afternoon at five o'clock, the broadside said," Clay told me.

"They might not come, of course," I said, trying to stay cool about it. "After last night, they might figure it was too dangerous."

"Or they might figure that it was a good way to get a line on us again," Clay suggested. "I mean, they'd figure if we saw that broadside, we'd know it was our horse, wouldn't they?"

I shook my head. "I'm not so sure. The thing

is, they don't know that we stopped in Big Top. So they wouldn't know that we know about the way they're using Liz."

"That's true," Clay said doubtfully. "On the other hand, it's not just every horse that's obviously saddle broke but won't let anyone ride her. They might think we'd figure it out."

"I guess it's worth a try, anyway," I agreed. "If they figure we don't know about Liz, then they probably won't see any danger in it. Either they'll show up or they won't."

"Right. Let's get out to the station. Once we're set up there, I'll go back to the hotel and leave a message for Charlie."

We approached the cattle pens carefully, just in case the rustlers had decided to try a repeat of last night. We didn't need to worry, though. Today there was plenty of activity. Cattle buyers were all over the place and so were a few men with cattle to sell.

"How should we play this?" I asked, taking in the scene.

"How much of a look at you do you figure those fellas got last night, Luke?"

"At a guess, none. When they grabbed me it was dark, and by the time it got light I was lying face down over a saddle. They sure didn't have much time to see me while I was riding away. I was covered with dust, anyway. I still am."

He nodded. "Yeah, and I don't think the ones I hired as hands back when you had the measles got much of a look at you, either. Which means that none of them is going to recognize you."

"So you think it might be a good idea if I just sit down on that bench over there against the station with this bag of doughnuts and keep an eye on what's going on?"

"With *part* of that bag of doughnuts," he corrected. "I'm hungry too. Other than that, you've got it right. If anyone shows any interest in our cattle, you come running and we'll follow them."

"You know, Clay, I've got a sort of idea about these cattle. We wanted to get them to the railhead, right?"

"Right."

"Well, that's where they are."

"So?"

"So let's sell 'em."

Clay got a real thoughtful look on his face. "For the life of me, Luke, I can't see any reason why we shouldn't do just that."

He brushed some of the dust off his sleeve and headed over toward the most prosperous-looking man in the crowd. I followed along behind, wondering if this was really such a good idea. Suppose the rustlers had already sold the cattle?

"Excuse me," Clay said, "but are you planning to buy any cattle?"

"I am if I can find out who this bunch here belongs to," the man said. Waving his hand toward the C Bar L cattle, he gave Clay a sharp look.

"That would be us," Clay told him.

The man frowned. "The railroad agent here told me that the man who brought them in was a tall redhead."

For some reason that rang a bell with me, but I couldn't quite place why.

"He's one of our hands," Clay said. "Want to see our tally book?"

"I certainly do."

Clay pulled out the little leather-covered notebook that was never very far from him and turned to the last few pages. On them was a tally of the roundup, along with a careful notation of every steer we'd lost on the trail. On the cover, burned into the leather, was a miniature copy of the brand on the hip of the cattle in the stock pens.

"All right," the man said, handing Clay back his book. "It doesn't hurt to be careful. My name's John Applegate."

"I'm Clay Peters. My partner is Luke Johnson."

"Nice to meet you," Applegate said, shaking

hands. "What were you thinking of getting for these cattle?"

"Thirty-five a head," Clay said promptly.

"What?" Applegate yelped. "That's railhead prices."

Clay looked around, surprised. "Looks like railhead to me."

"I couldn't go higher than twenty-five," Applegate said flatly.

Clay let his gaze wander over toward some of the other buyers. Starting to sense what was going on, they were drifting in our direction.

"All right, twenty-eight," Applegate said generously.

I figured right then that we had him. Whenever the other fella tops his own offer without giving you a chance to say anything, then you're in the saddle.

Clay still didn't say anything, but one of the other buyers did. "I can go thirty," he said. "And I've got it right here in cash."

"I was going to say thirty," Applegate protested angrily.

"Then you should have," Clay said. "It's already been said now. The question is, are you going to say anything higher?"

Applegate hesitated, then shook his head. "That's top price here. I'll wait for another herd."

Clay turned his attention to our buyer. "I

guess you've got yourself a deal, mister. Let's tally them up."

"Sure thing," the buyer said, beaming. "I thought I wasn't going to get a chance at anything until Applegate had gotten all he wanted. The name's Pilgrim, by the way. Amos Pilgrim."

"Well, Mr. Pilgrim," I said, "you know how to do it now."

When we got the pen agent out of his office, he didn't seem to have any trouble accepting that we owned the herd. "I guess that's why your man went off without signing his receipt," he said.

My blood ran a little cold at that. If we'd had to produce a copy of the receipt to turn those cattle over to Pilgrim, we'd have been in trouble. As it was, though, we went through paperwork without a hitch.

After that we headed out to the pens to start the tally. The chute between the first of the pens with our cattle was opened as Clay and Mr. Pilgrim took up positions at either side of it. At their signal a few boys started pushing the cattle out through the chute into the empty pen on the other side of the yards. It took a while, but at the end of two hours we had our count.

"I make it six hundred and forty-nine," Pilgrim said.

"I get six forty-eight," Clay told him. "I guess it'd be fair to go with my count."

"You're a gentleman, sir," Pilgrim said. "I suggest that we go back to the office and settle up. And then, I think, a drink might be in order."

Clay and I didn't have any fault to find with that program, so that's what we did. Pilgrim was as good as his word, and he had the money right there. The agent witnessed the transaction, and then the three of us left.

"I got it out of the bank this morning," Pilgrim said. "I've been losing out to Applegate for the last week, and I thought if I could offer cash, it might give me an edge. Applegate would have had to wire for his."

Pilgrim got his horse, and we headed back into town along the main street.

"I think," Clay said, "that I'd better meet you two at the saloon a little later. I want to turn this money in for a draft on the bank. It's a little too much to be carrying around. And I think I'd better get back to the hotel and tell Charlie what we've been up to. He might be getting a little worried about now."

"Yeah," I agreed. "I'd sort of forgotten he was going to meet us there. I'll just go along with Mr. Pilgrim. There are a few things about that herd he might be interested in."

Clay turned and walked off, and I turned to Mr. Pilgrim.

"I guess you might have some idea what the best saloon is," I said. "You've certainly been in town awhile longer than I have."

"Wouldn't make a bit of difference," he told me. "I know where the best saloon is after I've been in a town ten minutes. It's a survival trait. You ought to get into that habit."

I grinned at him. "Lead the way," I said.

Chapter Thirteen

I didn't want to tell Mr. Pilgrim too much, but I didn't want to tell him too little, either. By the time I finished my story and my beer, he knew that some rustlers had shown an unhealthy interest in those cattle, and he'd decided that it might be a good idea to keep a guard on them until they were shipped.

"Sounds like you had a rough trip," he said, draining the last of his drink. He looked around to see if he could catch the bartender's eye.

"I've been on worse," I told him, which was true enough. "The thing is that those rustlers did get a few of our horses, so I'll be keeping an eye out to see if any of them show up around the cattle. If you catch sight of anyone who shows more interest than he ought to, I'd appreciate hearing about it."

"Sure thing, although I expect to be shipping tomorrow. Say, what do you think is keeping that partner of yours?"

143

Well, I thought that was a pretty good question myself. I shook my head. "I guess maybe I'd better go and find out, Mr. Pilgrim." I stood up. "It's been a pleasure," I said, shaking his hand. "Maybe we'll see you again next year."

"I'll look forward to it," he told me.

I headed for the End of the Line Hotel, hoping that Clay would be there. I didn't really have any reason to think he wouldn't be, but nothing had gone according to plan in so long that I was getting a little nervous.

"I'm Luke Johnson," I told the clerk at the desk. "You ought to have a room for me."

"Ought to?" he said with a raised eyebrow. "This is quite a busy hotel, sir. We have quite a number of guests."

I decided I might as well keep my temper. "Rooms were booked for us yesterday," I said patiently. "You want to check?"

I could see he really didn't want to. I had a feeling I was just a touch dustier than he liked his guests to be. On the other hand, I probably looked nearly as mean as I did dusty.

"Yes, sir, I believe we do have something. Room 225. That's up the stairs and on the left."

"What about Clay Peters?"

"Right next door—room 227."

I took the key and headed up the stairs. Once I found Clay I was going to get into some clean clothes or maybe take a nap. They both sounded like good ideas, and I was trying to decide which one sounded best as I knocked on the door of Clay's room.

I waited a minute, but there was no answer. I didn't bother to knock again, just tried the door. It swung open easily, and I stepped through with a sinking feeling in my stomach and my gun in my hand.

Someone had been in there, all right. From the look of the place it had been a couple of someones and they hadn't been real friendly. Stuff was scattered from one end of the room to the other. Clay's saddlebags were thrown over next to the bed, so it was a pretty good guess that he'd been one of the people in the room.

I stood there trying to think what to do. My brain seemed a little numb. I had about three different ideas and I just couldn't decide which was the right one. Before I had a chance to sort them out, the door opened again behind me. I spun around and came within an inch of putting a bullet right between Charlie's eyes.

"Whoa!" he said in alarm. "Take it easy, Luke. What's going on here?"

I lowered the gun as his eyes took in the room. "Where's Clay?" he asked.

"I'd say he's about twenty minutes on his way to wherever I was headed," I said.

"Let's go, then." He spun toward the door.

"You want to just hold on a minute," I snapped.

"We haven't got any time to waste," he protested.

"I think we'd better make a little time. This needs some thinking."

"What's there to think about? They've got Clay, and we've got to get him back."

"Look, they had me and we got me back, and it didn't really get us all that far, did it? We have to use our heads here. I heard that bunch talking before I escaped. As long as they just have one of us, they aren't going to take the chance of killing him."

"Are you planning to just let them have Clay for the rest of his life?"

Charlie was beginning to get on my nerves just the least little bit. "Look here," I said. "I don't mind too much when Clay starts running off in what looks like six different directions. He knows what he's doing. I don't know whether you do or not. So if you don't mind, I'm going to think about this a little. If you want to go racing around, you do it, but until I'm sure I can get Clay out safely, I'm not going to go running into any lions' dens."

I don't think he liked that much. "All right," he finally said. "Are you planning on going to the law?"

"Nope. Once the law is into it, they wouldn't

have any reason to keep Clay alive. I kind of think I'll be hearing from them pretty soon."

"You're probably right. But look here—they don't know me, and maybe while you're waiting here I can take a look around and see if I can find Clay. Even if they caught me at it, they still couldn't kill either of us with you loose."

"All right, but don't take too many chances. They probably wouldn't kill both of you with me loose, but they wouldn't have to keep both of you."

He gulped a little, nodded, then started toward the door. "Will you be waiting here?"

"I might go back down to the stockyard. Could be I'll be able to pick up a trail there. Someone might know where these guys are camped."

"But you won't go out after them by yourself, will you?"

I shook my head.

"All right, then. I'll see you later."

He left, and I sat down on the bed and stared at my feet. I still wasn't sure what I ought to do, but I knew that I wasn't about to go running off half-cocked like Charlie. There was something here I didn't quite understand, and I wanted to work it out.

To begin with, I decided, these fellas didn't know we had sold the herd. As far as they were concerned, everyone in this town but us thought they were legitimate cattlemen. Now, if they were only interested in selling the herd and making a profit, why didn't they just kill us, sell the herd, and go? True, they might have been afraid that if they didn't get both of us at once, the other one would call in the law, but on the other hand, it had taken us only two hours to find a buyer, count the cattle, and collect our money. The rustlers could have done the same and been out of there as slick as a whistle.

Which meant, I decided, that they didn't want to just take the money and run. They were planning to come back again with other herds and they wanted their names to be clean. This wasn't a one-time deal. Well, that fit in with what we knew, all right. That sheriff a few towns back had said that ours wasn't the first herd that had been rustled, and he'd also said that Clay was the first one to come out of it alive.

"All right," I muttered under my breath. "So they aren't going to do anything to make themselves look bad if they can help it."

That gave me an edge if I could just figure out how to use it. And then I remembered that I had another edge. At five o'clock they were still going to put on their little exhibition with Liz, or at least I hoped they were. They didn't have any better idea of how I looked than they ever had, and with any luck I could follow them back and then get some help to bust Clay out.

I guess that as a plan it wasn't much, but I was tired and my head was hurting again. Besides, it was all the plan I had. I turned it around for a minute more without thinking of anything else and finally realized that if I wanted to be any good for anything, I'd better take a nap. Clay had been right. Getting knocked unconscious isn't much of a substitute for a good night's sleep.

Chapter Fourteen

I woke up around four and lay in bed wondering where I was and what I was doing there. In a minute it all came back to me and I wished that it hadn't. I lay there for another minute, trying to decide whether I should get something to eat before the bronc riding, when there was a knock on the door. I got up and opened it.

"Are you Luke Johnson?" a skinny kid about twelve years old asked.

"That's right."

"I've got a message for you." He held out a grubby piece of paper.

"Who'd you get it from?" I asked, unfolding it.

"A guy out in the street gave me a nickel to bring it to you."

"I don't suppose he was going to wait for an answer?"

"Nope. He left right off."

151

"Okay," I said, fishing in my pocket for another nickel. "Thanks a lot, kid."

He took the nickel and left, and I stood in the doorway looking at that note. It didn't say too much, just ordered me to make out a bill of sale for all the cattle down in the cattle pens. Once I'd done that, they'd be glad to let Clay loose. They even told me where to leave it.

I'd have been happy to try it, just to see the looks on their faces when they found out the cattle had already been sold, but I knew that I'd be signing Clay's death warrant right along with the bill of sale. I thought again about going to the law. Finally, I had something concrete to show a sheriff.

On the other hand, I already had a plan. I decided to stick with it.

I went down to the dining room to try for an early supper, stopping at the desk to see if Charlie had returned. He hadn't.

I ate quick and light and then headed out for the bronc busting. The closer I got to it, the higher my blood pressure rose. Liz had been mine since the day she was foaled, and in all that time she'd never let anyone else ride her. I'd taught her that when she was just a filly and my brother had shown signs of trying to borrow her on occasion. Since then I'd once gotten her to let Clay on her back with me leading her, and apparently she'd also let Ben ride her.

She was pretty handy at getting rid of un-
wanted guests, but it was a lot of work that she
shouldn't have to do.

I got Binny from the stable and saddled him
up. I wanted to be able to follow them fast if I
needed to. Then I headed out.

I wasn't the first one there. A crowd of
about fifteen men had gathered near the livery-
stable corral where the festivities were supposed to take place, and from the way they
were talking, this wasn't the first time those
rustlers had tried this.

"I'll tell you that pony acts saddle-broke to
me," one guy said, shaking his head stub-
bornly.

"Not when there's anyone *in* the saddle,"
another insisted. "The minute anyone puts
some weight on her, she cuts loose."

"I reckon she's smart enough not to waste
any time fighting a saddle," a third man said.

A big, swaggering sort of man snorted.
"There you go again. Next thing you know,
you'll be saying that mare ain't never going to
be rode."

"I suppose *you're* going to ride her," the first
guy said.

"Darn right I am. I could use a hundred dollars."

"Does it seem to you they'd offer a hundred

dollars if they expected to have to pay it out?" I asked.

"They just figure they aren't going to find any real men in a town this size," the man said, swinging around toward me.

It occurred to me that if this fella was a sample, they were probably right, but I guessed it wouldn't be too smart to say so.

There was a commotion at the other side of the crowd and then a whinny that I would have recognized anywhere. I started toward it, realizing that Liz had caught my scent. I was halfway through the crowd before I stopped myself.

I couldn't get too near Liz. If I did, it'd be clear she knew me, and that would be the end of my advantage. I moved off to the side of the crowd, where I could get a good look at what was going on without being too close.

There she was, her little chestnut nose raised, sniffing the air, trying to figure out where I was. I'd gotten downwind, hoping she wouldn't spot me again, but I wasn't sure if I was far enough away. As she tugged on her reins I took a good look at the man who was holding them.

And I froze. I'd seen that guy before and he'd seen me. Big and tall and redheaded, just like the station agent had said, it was Cort Hanson, the man who'd offered to race his horse against Binny back in Sanford Junction. And he'd recognize me as easily as I'd just spotted him.

I tipped my hat down low over my face and stepped back into the shadows of the livery stable. This was going to be a whole lot trickier than I'd thought. I had to be able to follow them away from here, and not only would Hanson recognize me but there was a good chance he'd recognize Binny too. After all, he'd wanted him bad enough to try to steal him after that race.

"All right, gents," Hanson said. "Who's gonna be first to eat some dust?"

"You're wasting your time, Hanson. Some horses ain't never been rode," an old-timer with long white whiskers said. "They'd rather die than let someone on their backs."

"True enough," Hanson agreed. "But this little mare isn't one of them. Take a look at her. This isn't just some mustang off the range. This mare has some blood in her. And as for not being rode— Come here, kid."

A skinny teenager stepped out of the crowd, and I had a notion that I was finally getting to see Ben.

"Now then," Hanson said. "Here's the kid who rode her the other day. I imagine he can ride her again. What do you say, kid? No hundred dollars this time, but I'll give you a dollar if you'll try it again."

The kid nodded solemnly and stepped forward. He took Liz's bridle and seemed surprised when she tossed her head impatiently. She was still scanning the crowd and sniffing the air, and I figured that she hadn't given up on me yet.

The kid took a firmer grip on her bridle and vaulted into the saddle. Liz turned her head just to make sure who it was, then turned her attention back to looking for me. He gave her a little nudge with his heels, and she obligingly stepped forward. He rode her around for a minute, then brought her back to where they'd started and slid out of the saddle.

Hanson tossed him a silver dollar and turned back to the crowd. "Now then," he said. "The mare can be ridden, she's just particular. Anybody think he can stay on for only two minutes?"

Well, of course, there was a lot of hesitation. No one wanted to get thrown after a kid had ridden her with no trouble at all. On the other hand, no one wanted to appear afraid to try something that a kid had done with no trouble at all.

After a minute, though, the big fella with the big mouth stepped forward and handed over his dollar.

"I guess I can ride her whether she likes it or not," he said. "She ain't much bigger'n a dog, anyway."

He took the reins and settled his rump into the saddle. Liz didn't even bother to check his looks. She just upended herself and a second later he was sitting in the dust.

Well, that brought a laugh from the crowd and quite a few more takers. Now that one man had been dumped, there wasn't quite so much pressure on the others, and they were all eager to give it a try.

None of 'em seemed to give Liz too much trouble. She tried something a little different on each of 'em, so that they couldn't be ready for her tricks. Well, I still wasn't any too happy, but at the same time I kind of enjoyed watching her dump everyone.

Then I stopped enjoying myself real sudden. A man who was a little different from the others stepped forward. For one thing, he had the coldest look I've ever seen. For another, the rowels on his spurs had been filed so sharp that they'd draw blood just touching a horse.

I started to step forward, then froze. I couldn't let that man ride Liz, but I had to. If I was recognized, that was the end of the only chance I had to find Clay.

The man held out his dollar, but as Hanson reached to take it, a small hand flew out and knocked it into the dust. Both men looked down in surprise at Ben, who stood there shaking his head. Hanson said something, but the head shook even more firmly and then Ben pointed down.

Hanson looked at the spurs, and I held my breath. Finally Hanson looked up again and said, "I don't believe I can let you take a try wearing those spurs, mister."

"Nothing was said about conditions," the man said coldly.

"Just the same, this mare is worth a lot of money to me, and whether she throws you or not those spurs could do quite a bit of damage."

"I guess you should have thought of that before," the man said, his voice getting softer and more dangerous.

Much as I would have liked to see him blow Hanson's head off, there was always the chance that Hanson would just back down.

"Come on!" I called, trying to disguise my voice. "If he's afraid to ride her without them mean-looking spurs, let somebody else take a chance."

A murmur of approval went through the crowd and a few others added their voices to mine. All eyes were on the two men, and so no one noticed Liz's sudden attention except maybe Ben, and he wasn't going to be telling anyone.

In another minute it was clear that if the man with the spurs wanted to have any face left at all, he was going to have to ride without them. He hesitated a second longer and then started taking them off.

As soon as he hit the saddle it was clear that he knew a lot about how to stay on a horse. He had the reins pulled so tight that Liz couldn't really get her head up. I held my breath, but I guess Liz had picked up a thing or two over the last few weeks. She didn't waste any time. She just kept her head turning right around and grabbed hold of one of his boots. She chomped on it, and the second he let up on the reins in surprise, she whipped her head around and had him half out of the saddle before he knew what was going on. After that, three crowhops finished what she'd started and she stood there, straddle-legged, breathing deeply and glaring down at him.

He glared right back as he got up from the ground, and he seemed inclined to take another try, but I guess Hanson figured he'd gotten about as much cash from the crowd as he was going to.

"Well, folks, I guess that's about it for today. Thanks for coming."

He turned and started to lead Liz over to

where his own horse was tied, but I guess the wind had shifted a little. She gave a snort and pulled away and suddenly there she was trotting through the crowd toward me.

I wanted to reach out and grab her reins, but I couldn't. Instead I turned and slid into the livery stable. I closed the door and turned to look back through a crack. Liz was poking her head at the door and trying to keep the reins out of Hanson's hand. Hanson was cursing and grabbing at them. Pretty near everyone else was laughing.

I guess Hanson didn't like that much. He took a grab at Liz and she took a grab at him. I don't know what Hanson would have done next, but Ben slid up beside them and grabbed Liz's reins. She still had it in mind to keep looking for me, but he managed to coax her away from the door, much to my relief.

I headed out the other side of the stable, to where I'd left Binny. Chances were that Hanson would be heading out to his camp now, and I didn't intend to be far behind. I might not be the world's best tracker, but the day I couldn't pick Liz's prints out of a whole herd would be a long time coming.

I eased Binny cautiously around the side of the livery stable and, sure enough, there was Hanson on his horse, leading Liz. Ben strolled along in more or less the same direction, like he wasn't going to join up with them later. I wondered why they bothered. It must have been pretty obvious to most of the crowd that the kid hadn't just happened along.

I kept well back even though the streets were fairly crowded. I didn't want either Hanson or Liz to know I was following. I wasn't sure how far off Hanson could recognize me, but I knew that once Liz got out of all the confusing smells in town, she'd be able to pick up either me or Binny pretty easily. Now that Hanson wasn't distracted, it might not take too long for him to notice that Liz was spotting someone familiar.

And now that I knew Hanson was involved, it was pretty obvious that he was going to take a guess that it was me. So unless I was pretty careful, I could end up walking right into their hands.

Chapter Fifteen

As soon as I was certain of Hanson's direction, I pulled up and waited for him to get a way ahead. Ben hadn't rejoined him yet, and I was beginning to think that I was wrong. Maybe Ben was planning to stay in town for a while.

That would probably be just as well, I thought as I rode out of town. Things might get a little rough, and it would be just as well if there wasn't a kid in the middle of it all.

I hoped that we'd get wherever we were going before it became too dark, but I wasn't counting on it. Because of that I didn't want to get too far behind. I might be able to track Liz in the daylight, but I sure wasn't going to be able to at night.

I rode for about an hour, not having any trouble with the tracks, when all of a sudden Binny's ears pricked up like he had heard something. I pulled him up, afraid we were getting too close, and listened. Sure enough, there was the sound of a horse's hooves. Only they weren't ahead of us, they were behind.

I turned Binny off the trail and into a stand of trees. I slid off and clamped a hand over his nose so that he wouldn't whinny a greeting. Horses aren't any too discriminating when it comes to strangers.

I waited quietly, figuring that it was probably the kid. He'd have had another horse in town and would be coming out to join the others. That was okay as long as he didn't spot me. I'd just wait until he went past, then fall in behind him.

Sure enough, a few seconds later a horse appeared around the bend in the trail. Or rather, two horses appeared.

That was a little bit of a surprise—particularly when I saw who the other fellow was. I took my hand off Binny's nose and led him out onto the trail.

The man gave a smothered oath and whipped out his gun.

"Forget it, Charlie," I said. "It's just me. I see you caught up with the kid."

For a minute he kept the gun pointing at me, then suddenly he let the barrel drop.

"You pretty nearly scared me to death," he said. "You ought to give a little warning."

He got off his horse and tossed the reins to

Ben. "Yeah," he said. "I saw Ben in town. I told him those guys were rustlers. I figured he could take me out to where Clay was."

"You were planning to go after them alone?" I asked.

"Well, I couldn't find you. I guess you couldn't find me, either."

Naturally enough, that stopped me. I hadn't even tried looking for him.

"Okay," I said. "I guess if Ben knows the way, this'll be a little easier. We can keep back far enough so there isn't any chance of being spotted, and we'll go in after dark."

Charlie nodded. "That sounds like a pretty good idea to me."

"Once he's shown us where their camp is, maybe we'd better send him back to town for the sheriff," I suggested.

Charlie looked doubtful. "Would that do any good? He can't talk, remember."

"He can carry a note, can't he?"

"Sure, but what do we say—'Follow this kid and he'll lead you to a bunch of rustlers'? I mean, they don't have the cattle out there or anything. We'll have to wait until they try to sell them, if they haven't already."

"That's no problem," I told him. "They've got Liz, which makes them horse thieves. As far as the cattle go, they won't be selling them, because Clay and I already did."

"You what?" Charlie said, looking thunder-struck.

"We sold them. Over at the cattle pens, we got to thinking. I mean, our cattle were right there waiting to be sold, and there were some men wanting to buy them. So it just seemed to make sense to go ahead and do it."

Charlie didn't say anything for a while. His mouth opened a few times like he was going to, but then it would shut again. Finally he said, "What did you do with the money?"

"Clay had the bank transfer it to our account back home."

"I'll be darned," he said.

"So really," I told him, "all we have to do is shake Clay and Liz loose, and we're home free. After that, the law can take care of Hanson and his bunch, for all I care."

"Hanson," he said with a curious note in his voice.

"The guy who has Liz," I explained. "I ran into him before. I just didn't know that he had anything to do with this bunch. I thought he was just a horse thief."

Ben had been listening to everything with great attention, but this was a little more than he could take, I guess. He urged his horse forward, reached down, and tapped me on the shoulder. I didn't know just what he wanted, of course, but I thought I could make a pretty good guess.

"The mare that Hanson has been using as his bucking bronco belongs to me," I explained. "I'd kind of like to get her back."

It was like some big light had dawned on the kid. He got a real thoughtful look on his face and backed off a little.

"Well, whoever it is, we'd better get riding," Charlie said.

I nodded agreement and swung into the saddle. I motioned Ben ahead. He gave me an odd look as he went past, and I guessed that he was wanting to tell me something and couldn't figure out how to get it across. I paused a second, waiting for Charlie, but he motioned me ahead.

We rode for another couple of hours, and it was starting to get a little dark when Ben pulled up and turned his horse back toward us.

"We must be getting close," Charlie said. "Should we wait here until it gets darker, Ben?"

Ben hesitated, but then nodded.

"Fine," I said. "I've got a few doughnuts left here, I think. Maybe we can have a little snack while we wait."

Nobody seemed to have any objection to that, so we found a good place that was out of sight of the trail and finished off the doughnuts.

By that time it was dark enough to move on, and I said as much.

"Seems like as good a time as any," Charlie agreed.

"Okay, then let's get this kid out of here. It could get dangerous."

"All right. Should we send him back to the hotel?"

I still thought that the sheriff wasn't such a bad idea, but, after all, Charlie knew more about Ben than I did. I guessed I'd better leave it to him.

"Okay," I said. "But if we aren't back by morning, I think he should try to find some help."

"Sounds fair enough," Charlie agreed. "I'll send him on his way."

He led Ben over to his horse and started giving him instructions while I threw a saddle back on Binny. I'd wanted to give him whatever breather I could. Chances were that he might have to do a little traveling tonight, and if we couldn't shake loose a horse for Clay he might be carrying double. Of course, I was planning to have Liz with us when we left, but I didn't want to leave anything to chance.

"Okay," Charlie said. "Let's ride."

"Do you have to sound so much like we're going to a tea party?" I said. "This could be a little dangerous."

"So could getting up in the morning," Charlie told me. "Come on. Ben says it's just over the next rise."

We rode forward cautiously and, sure enough, once we'd passed the crest of the rise we could make out a little fire flickering between some rocks a way ahead by the side of the trail.

"Guess it might be a good idea if one of us was to circle around," I whispered.

"I'll do it," Charlie said quietly. "Give me about ten minutes."

"All right. Just be careful."

We separated. I headed off the trail, then dismounted and started moving quietly toward the rocks. When I'd gotten close enough, I tied Binny to a bush and eased forward on foot.

There was a rock that looked like it would give me pretty good cover, and it was only about twenty feet from the fire. As I got nearer, I could see that most of the activity in the camp was on the other side of the fire, so I moved into position behind the rock without too much trouble.

Once there, I took a good look around. On the far side of the fire, Cort Hanson was standing with a plate of something in one hand and a fork in the other. He was gesturing with the fork, and from the look on his face I guessed that he was telling the others about what had happened in town. There were three men sitting around the fire, and, a little way off, leaning against a rock, was another man. The light wasn't real good, but it took me only a second to see that the last man was Clay.

I lay there behind the rock until I was pretty sure that Charlie would be in position. Then I eased up onto my knees and lined up my rifle on Cort Hanson's chest.

"All right," I called out. "Everyone freeze."

That got their attention, all right. Hanson's hand started toward his gun, and then he thought better of it. One of the others dropped his plate of food with a clatter.

"All right, now," I said. "You're covered from two directions. Charlie, you want to let these guys know you're out there?"

"Sure thing, Luke," Charlie said.

I guess that should have made me feel a lot more secure. And it probably would have if Charlie hadn't been speaking from right behind me, and if he hadn't had a gun poked in the back of my head.

Chapter Sixteen

Getting a shock like that makes you feel about the same as having a mule kick you right in the gut. For a little while all you can do is try to get your breath back. It wasn't like I'd been even the least bit suspicious of Charlie. Before I'd had a chance to do more than take a deep breath, he was hauling me onto my feet and yanking the rifle away from me.

"What took you so long?" Hanson called, starting forward. "We were expecting you to ride in with him all trussed up."

"I figured you guys could do some of the work for a change," Charlie said. "I don't know what the blazes you think I pay you for." He shoved the gun into the small of my back, and I started moving forward. There might be something I could do to get out of this mess, but right now I was having enough trouble dealing with the fact that not only was Charlie in with them but he was apparently the boss.

171

"Put your hands behind your neck, Luke," Charlie said, "and move over there next to Clay."

I did what he said. Clay sat there looking up at me and shrugged. "He brought me out here the same way yesterday after I left the bank," he told me.

"Pipe down," Hanson snapped. He gave me a shove, and I wound up on the ground next to Clay. While I was considering returning the favor, one of the others grabbed my wrist and the next thing I knew I was trussed up like a Christmas turkey.

"All right," Charlie said. "Now we've got some thinking to do."

"What's there to think about?" Hanson asked. "We've got them both. All we have to do is shoot them and get on with selling the herd."

"Unfortunately, it's not quite that simple," Charlie snapped. "They already sold it."

"Huh?"

"You heard me. This morning they went down to the cattle pens, found a buyer, and made a deal. Then they had the bank transfer the funds to their hometown."

Hanson seemed frozen. "You mean we did this all for nothing?" he said finally.

"That's what we have to think about," Charlie told him. "There's got to be a way to get that money, but we can't kill them yet."

That seemed like pretty good news to me.

"I don't think you can expect all that much help from us," Clay told him, "unless the deal includes a way for us to come out of it alive."

That sounded even better.

Charlie looked down at us and nodded. "I guess not," he muttered. "All right, then. You got any ideas?"

"You're not going to listen to them, are you?" Hanson asked, sounding surprised. "I mean, they can identify us."

"If you can think of any way for us to get that money without their help, I'm willing to listen," Charlie said.

"It must still be in the bank," Hanson said. "There wouldn't have been time for the bank to have sent it anywhere yet. We could just rob the place."

Charlie looked like he was counting to ten. "If I'd wanted to be a bank robber, Cort, I wouldn't have gone to all the trouble of stealing those cattle. The beauty of my plan was that people wouldn't know we were doing it, remember? I'd like to be able to go on with my life just the way it is."

"Well, I don't know how you expect to be able to do that if these two guys, who can identify you, are walking around loose. We have to kill them."

"Maybe we do, Cort," Charlie snarled, "but it might be a little bit smarter not to keep telling 'em so."

Hanson shut up like a trap, and Charlie turned back to us. "The thing is," he said, "that Cort is right. If you want a deal, you're going to have to come up with a way that leaves you alive and keeps you from turning us in too."

Nobody said anything for a minute. "How about a contract?" I said.

"What?"

"You know, we all sign a paper saying that we're giving you the money of our own free will to buy something or other from you. Then if we try to say you stole it, it'll just look like we had second thoughts about going through with it."

Hanson shook his head. "What about the cattle? You could still say we stole them."

"How far would that get us?" Clay asked. "We're the ones who sold every blessed head of 'em. The fact is that you guys haven't done so well. About all we could prove is that you drove the cattle to market for us and we didn't even have to pay your wages."

Charlie was frowning a little. "It could work," he said finally. "If you can figure out something in the contract that we could be selling you. Something that looks good enough for a court."

"What about the mine?" Hanson suggested suddenly.

"What mine?" I asked.

"We bought a played-out mine shaft a few months ago," Charlie said. "This is mining country, and we needed to have something to give us a little cover around here. We didn't want it to look like we were just hanging around." He thought a minute. "I guess that just might do it. A mine could bring that much money, and if it proved to be worthless— Well, that's the sort of risk you take when you buy a mine."

I let out a breath I hadn't realized I'd been holding.

"All right, then," Charlie said. "In the morning we'll ride into town with Peters. He put the money in the bank, so he can handle all of the signing that's needed. We'll do up the deed. After that we'll let Johnson go."

"One other thing," I said.

"Yeah?"

"This deal had better include Liz."

"Who the heck is Liz?" Hanson asked.

"The mare you've been parading around all over the place. Haven't you got any better sense than to put a horse you stole on public display?" Charlie said.

"I want her back," I persisted.

Hanson shook his head. "I've made a lot of money with her. I'd sooner keep her."

"No horse, no deal," I told them.

"You'll get your mare," Charlie said impatiently. "I suggest we break this up now. I'm hungry and I'm tired. We'll finish in the morning."

He turned and walked away, and the others followed him.

"You know, Luke," Clay said softly, "I wouldn't count too much on this deal, with or without Liz. I don't think they really intend to let us go."

"Neither do I," I told him. "I just figured Charlie wouldn't think we meant it if I didn't kick up a little fuss about Liz."

"Yeah, I guess so," Clay agreed. "He's heard you talking about her for long enough. Got any ideas for us getting out of here alive?"

"Well, that kid Ben was supposed to bring help in the morning if we didn't get back to town, but I'm sure that's not really what Charlie told him to do."

Clay nodded.

"So I guess maybe the only thing is for you to wait until you get into town, with a lot of people around, and make a break for it," I told him. "Chances are they won't shoot you with witnesses present, and maybe you can get to the sheriff."

"And what happens to you?"

"Well, ideally, you'll get back out here before they blow my head off."

"It's a nice thought, Luke, but I don't imagine the odds on that are any too good."

"I'm open to a better plan if you've got one."

"How about if I refuse to go into town unless you come too."

I thought it over, but I couldn't see any way they'd go for it. "They'll never buy it, Clay. They know they're walking a pretty thin line. They might just decide to cut their losses, meaning us, and forget about the money. This contract idea has bought us a little time, but I guess that's all."

"We've got all night to think about it," Clay said encouragingly. "I don't know why it is, but I'm not real sleepy."

Neither was I, and I tossed around for fifteen or twenty minutes, trying to get comfortable. The fact is that that's not too easy to do when you're tied up.

I guess Clay wasn't doing any too well, either. After a while he said in a low voice, "You still awake, Luke?"

"Like you said, Clay, I don't think we're going to be doing a lot of sleeping tonight."

"Yeah, well . . . look, Luke, the thing is that I

don't know how likely it is that both of us will get out of this alive. So maybe. . . ."

I waited, but whatever he'd been going to say seemed to have gotten stuck a little. "Look, Clay," I said, "I don't know what you want to say, but you'd better say it before you leave for town."

He took a deep breath. "It's Breen, Luke. If you should get out of this and I don't, I want you to take care of her."

Well, I didn't quite know what to say to that. Breen needs taking care of just about as much as Clay does. Also, I couldn't see any way at all that I was going to get out of this alive if Clay didn't. I guessed, though, that that wasn't what Clay wanted to hear.

"Sure thing, Clay," I told him.

He was quiet for a minute, then he said, "We should have gotten married before I left. Breen wanted a big wedding and all, but. . . . "

"Look here, Clay, I know how you feel about Breen."

"Do you, Luke? Sometimes I'm not so sure *I* even know. She's not like anyone else I've ever met. She's so . . . I mean, I know I asked you to take care of her and all, but I know she probably wouldn't let you, and I know she probably wouldn't need any taking care of, anyway. I always thought that a woman should be soft and need a man to—well, you know what I mean. And now here's Breen and she's nothing like that at all, but I don't think I could ever love anybody like I love her."

That wasn't much of a surprise to me, but it was an awful lot more than I'd ever heard Clay say before.

"Don't worry, Clay," I told him. "We'll get back there. I've never missed a wedding yet."

That was all Clay said about Breen, but I guess it was on his mind. We did a little talking and a little planning, but his mind didn't really seem to be on it. By the time dawn broke, the only thing we'd been able to come up with was to take it as it came and see what happened.

Charlie didn't look a lot more rested than we were, and he didn't bother with any breakfast. He grabbed a cup of coffee, then came over and untied Clay.

"All right," he said. "Here's the way it's going to be. Cort and you, and me and Pete there are going to ride into town now. We'll get someone to draw up that deed, and then we'll go to the bank and get the money. The other two are going to be out here with Johnson. As soon as we get back here with the money we'll let Johnson and you go."

Clay looked like he was thinking of protesting, but then he shrugged and nodded. Maybe he'd think of something on the way. And maybe he wouldn't.

They rode out, and I was left there to stare at the two guards. One of them poured himself a cup of coffee and sat there blinking at the fire. The other one just rolled back into his blankets and went to sleep. I guess I didn't look like much of a threat.

I was considering asking for a cup of that coffee when I noticed that the guy wasn't really drinking it. In fact, when I looked really closely, it seemed like he was just about asleep. That cheered me up for a minute until I realized that they could both be flat out unconscious and it wasn't going to do me any good. Clay and I had spent a part of the night figuring out that there was no way we could get those ropes untied.

After a while the guard put down the cup of coffee, leaned back against a rock, and pulled his hat down over his eyes. In a few minutes he was snoring.

I sat there and turned ideas over in my head. I'd gotten to the point of wondering if I could crawl away into the rocks far enough so they couldn't find me when I felt a feather-light touch on my arm.

I jumped, but I managed to keep my mouth shut. A second later a knife started sawing away at the ropes on my wrists.

As soon as the ropes parted I swiveled around and found myself looking right into

Ben's mild blue eyes. Somehow, the idea of him taking a hand in this hadn't even crossed my mind, but I can't say I was sorry to see him there.

I held out my hand for the knife, and once he'd given it to me I pointed back the way he must have come. There was a chance that one of those two guards was going to wake up before I got out of there, and I didn't want them spotting Ben.

It took me about two seconds to cut the ropes on my ankles, and then I followed Ben. I got out through the rocks and stood there staring in amazement. There was Ben, and with him he had two saddled horses—Binny and Liz.

Liz spotted me and raised her nose to whinny a greeting, but Ben was too quick for her. He clamped a hand over her nostrils and I moved forward to help him keep her quiet. She stuck her nose out to me and I ran my hand down it, realizing suddenly what a difference it made having her back.

I took a deep breath and turned toward Ben. "You wait here," I said in a low voice. "I've got to do something about those two before they notice I'm gone."

I saw that Binny's saddle scabbard had my rifle in it, and I reached out and grabbed it.

Alarm flared in Ben's face and he grabbed my arm as he shook his head.

Seemed like he was a pretty peaceable sort of kid. "Don't worry," I said. "I won't shoot 'em. I'll just tie 'em up so they can't follow us. Okay?"

He released my arm and nodded, and I turned back to the camp.

I had a feeling that Charlie wasn't going to be any too happy with his guards. They were still sleeping, and it took me about five minutes to wake them up and tie them up against the same boulder where they'd had Clay and me. They said a few uncomplimentary things about my ancestry, but I didn't see any reason to let that get under my skin, all things considered.

"Now then, Ben," I said, going back to where I'd left him, "I guess we'd better head for town. Clay might just need a little help too."

Chapter Seventeen

When we got to town I figured that Clay and the others were maybe an hour ahead of us. That meant they could be at the bank or they could still be getting the papers drawn up.

"Ben," I said, turning to my silent companion, "do you think you could get the sheriff over to the bank?"

Ben nodded with great emphasis. Apparently he hadn't much liked it when Charlie had told me that no one would pay any attention to him.

"Okay," I said. "Then that's what I want you to do. I don't know whether Clay and the others will be there when you get there, but try to keep the sheriff around until they arrive." I stopped and frowned. "Those other horses from our remuda are still out there, aren't they? Because, right now, about the only thing we can do is prove that they're horse thieves."

He nodded.

"Good. Then we're in business. Let's go."

He headed one way, and I headed the other, toward the bank. I figured that was as good a place to start looking as any.

I went up to the door carefully. I didn't want anyone to get nervous and start shooting at this point.

I looked in, and there they were. I could just see Clay sitting there at a desk and signing something. Seemed like I was just in time. A little while longer and we'd have met them on the way back.

I walked in as quietly as I could. It was Clay who first spotted me, and the look on his face was a sight I wasn't going to forget soon.

"Clay," I said, "I've changed my mind. I don't believe we ought to buy that mine, after all."

"Whatever you say, Luke," he said real fast, his hand straying down to the empty holster at his side.

Hanson started to move toward me, but my holster had something in it, and as soon as I pulled it out, he froze.

"What's going on here?" the bank official snapped, not looking like he was real happy with whatever it was.

"Just a little mix-up about some money and some cattle and some horses," I told him soothingly. "The sheriff's on his way over. He'll get it all straightened out."

"Aren't you forgetting that you can't prove anything?" Charlie said.

"I don't think so," I told him. "In the first place, you've still got a few stolen horses out at your camp. In the second place, there's a witness to most of what you did, a witness you've sort of forgotten about."

"You're crazy," he snapped.

"Oh, yeah?" I said, gesturing toward the door, where Ben was just walking in with a well-armed and alert-looking sheriff. "How do you think I got loose, anyway?"

Charlie turned white, and I guessed that probably Ben knew plenty about his activities.

Clay got up from his chair and ran a hand through his hair. "Do you think Ben might like to come live on a ranch?" he asked me.

"I guess we could ask him," I said. I looked around and saw that Ben had left the bank. The sheriff strode forward, and Clay started to explain things to him. I headed for the door.

Outside, Liz was tied at the rack where I'd left her. Ben was stroking her ears while tears ran down his face.

As I moved forward to ask him if he'd be interested in a new home, somehow I didn't have any doubt that his answer would be yes.